The Beachcomber

Jack Mahan and Operation Yellow Jacket

by Bill D Rose

Dorrance Publishing Co
585 Alpha Drive
Pittsburgh, PA 15238
Visit our website at www.dorrancebookstore.com

ISBN: 978-1-4809-8686-2
eISBN: 978-1-4809-9206-1

The Beachcomber

Jack Mahan and Operation Yellow Jacket

Acknowledgements

Who would not want to live the carefree life of a beachcomber? My love of the beach, saltwater fishing, and the Coast Guard inspired my imagination to create the Mahan family and the Swordfish Marina. Many thanks to my wife Cathy, who helped me through some hard parts, and our friend Diane who proofed the manuscript at least five times.

The book is an action-adventure novel for mature readers. If it were a movie, it would be rated PG.

Part One –

The Swordfish Marina

Chapter 1

In 1958, somewhere in the oil fields of the Permian Basin, Marge and Bud Mahan were trying to keep alive. Bud was unemployed, had little money, and had no options for work other than on an oil rig risking his life for four hundred dollars per month. Bud's problem was the combination of drinking and gambling and Marge's problem was she loved Bud.

He was the type of individual that either had a lot of cash in his pocket or none at all. When he had money, he was generous beyond belief. When that ran dry, he would start drinking. Marge held the marriage together by keeping things positive and working as a cook at the local cafeteria.

Disappointingly, children were not part of their lives. The doctors said it was a problem with Marge. However the need to be around kids was somewhat satisfied by their home becoming the neighborhood part-time daycare center, kids called them Uncle Bud and Aunt Marge.

As it goes with most gamblers when he hit a dry spell he would tend to elevate the stakes of the game, resulting in either getting him well quickly or dead broke just as quick. Bud heard through the grapevine that a large crowd of big-time gamblers was meeting for a Las Vegas-style event at the Midland Country Club ballroom on the upcoming Saturday and Sunday. It was open to the public so anyone could attend. Of course these types of games were illegal but who cared, it was Texas in the Fifties. It would attract characters from all around. Some would even fly in to attend. He expected to see the local, seasoned oil men, the not-so-seasoned wildcatters, auto dealers, bankers, and maybe even a judge. They would have as many tables as necessary with each table having a dealer and up to six players. The game would be Seven Card Stud with a twenty-five dollar ante and no limit on the size of a bet. If a player could not match the wager, he would lose. After two hours, the tables would close. Then the players would move to other tables and start again. The games would begin at 6:00 PM Saturday and run twenty-four hours, closing down at 6:00 on Sunday. A player could walk away at any time.

To say the least, Bud was in a tizzy. At dinner that evening, he mentioned this to Marge. She knew that setting her foot down with a "no, you are not going," would not work.

She frowned at him and said, "What do you want me to say?"

Bud smiled and responded, "It would be nice to say, 'Okay, go on and have a good time'."

"No, I am not going to say that."

"How about I go and just watch for a little while?"

Marge put her hands on her hips and said, "I can't control what you do."

Laughing he said, "Oh, yes you can."

With a twinkle in her eye she reached into the pantry, selected an old coffee can, and removed the plastic cap. She pulled out a wad of money, counted out two hundred dollars, and gave it to him.

"When you lose this, come home," then she kissed him.

Bud smiled and said, "I'll bring you back a ton of gold and silver. Thanks, I love you too."

The next two days passed as slowly as Christmas to a kid. To keep himself busy, Bud did all the housework for Marge. As he moved into the bedroom, which they also used as an office, he did the unthinkable. Opening the file cabinet where all the significant documents were stored, he raffled through each file and found the home and life insurance papers, doctor's records, car titles and there it was, the deed to the house.

He paused and thought, *should I take it?* He could see a situation where it might save a winning hand. *Yes*, he thought, *I will only use it as insurance*. Then he thought, *Marge will kill me*! He closed the drawer without the deed.

It was finally Saturday afternoon, Marge had gone grocery shopping and he was dressing in his best suit. As he bent down to tie his shoes, he found himself staring at the file cabinet. Just as he was putting the car keys in his pocket, he quickly opened the file and grabbed the deed.

Bud arrived at the country club and signed in at the table just outside the hall. He casually strolled into the room and saw a couple of people he knew. Saying hello, he shook their hands and they each wished the other the best of luck. Soon the PA system announced the names of each player and their assigned table number. Finding the table and taking a seat, he felt nervous and edgy. He was a stranger sitting at a table with other strangers. He put his hands on the table and thought, *I can do this. I am damn good at Seven Card Stud.*

After placing the twenty-five dollar ante in the middle of the table, Bud sat back and waited for the dealer. Each player was dealt two cards face down (called the Hole Cards) and one card face-up. After every player looked at their Hole Cards the first round began. The first player to the dealer's left placed a bet of twenty-five dollars.

Each player matched the amount until the player sitting next to Bud announced, "I will accept your bet and up it an additional fifty dollars."

Looking again at his two Hole Cards, which did not match well, Bud folded and thought, *Okay, it was just twenty-five dollars to get a look*. He pushed his cards into the center of the table and set back with his arms crossed to watch the betting tendencies of each player.

This round continued with another player dropping out, leaving four players competing for the cash. After dealing three more cards, the pot had grown to more than three hundred dollars. On the final draw, the card was placed face down so other players could not see. To win, a player selects the best five-card poker hand out of his seven cards. The winning hand was three Jacks. The dealer raked in the money from the middle of the table, gave it to the happy gambler, then began to shuffle the deck for a new round

Interesting, Bud thought, *I am beginning to get comfortable*.

The first two-hour session came to a close and Bud's initial two hundred dollars had grown to two hundred and seventy-five. As midnight arrived, Bud's winnings were slowly growing but considering that he had lost one hand that cost him one hundred and fifty dollars, he was happy to still be in the game. At the next table change, Bud met some fascinating players but none quite as intriguing as a crusty old man from the Gulf Coast they called Snake.

Trying to figure him out a little, Bud asked, "You traveled a long way to be here, why?"

Snake answered, "I am tired of putting up with the Sport Fisherman. I'm selling my marina and moving back to Midland. I was born and raised here and I want to come home."

"Well, that doesn't tell me why you are here gambling."

"Son, that is none of your business."

"You are right, sir. Good luck."

The old man was a pretty good poker player. He won more hands that he lost. The dealer started a new round and Bud covertly stared at the old man's eyes. He watched Snake look at his Hole Cards and noticed a twitch and a slight glint in his eyes. Bud refocused on his hand by barely lifting just the corner of his hold cards. Two threes were silently staring back at him.

Promising, he thought.

The next card was dealt face-up. An ace was showing for Snake, a king for Bud, prompting a twenty dollar bet by Snake.

The game proceeded routinely with all other players dropping out, leaving only Snake versus Bud. Three more cards were dealt face up, with Snake betting an additional twenty dollars for each card. When the dealer announced the last face-up card, the fireworks began as Snake drew another Ace and Bud an additional three. Remembering his hole cards, he was looking at a three of a kind with one more card left to see.

Bud was now focusing on Snake's hand. He thought, *I have a lot of possibilities. I am setting on a winning hand unless he has another ace in his hole cards. If so, it would make a full house.* Snake bet another twenty dollars. Continuing his reasoning, he thought, *But if he did have a hidden ace, why did he open the bidding with a measly bet of only twenty dollars? He probably has only two pair. I will certainly stay for another draw.*

Bud met the bet and waited for the next card.

"Last card," the dealer said and dealt it down.

Bud had not even looked at his new hole card when Snake said, "I bet all I have." He counted his money and proudly pushed two thousand and fifteen dollars out to the middle of the table.

He was reaching to rake in the pot when Bud said, "Wait, I haven't looked at my new hole card." At this time, he knew that the old man hit his full house, probably three aces and two Kings. Slowly Bud looked at the card and froze for a moment while forcing himself to be calm. He couldn't believe it... Another three! A four of a kind which would beat Snake's full house! He knew that Snake would have no idea of his hand as three of the four threes were his hole cards.

He put his hand down and said to the old man, "Just where is your marina and how much is it worth?"

Not knowing what was about to happen Snake said, "The Tip of Texas, Port Isabell. It is worth one hundred thousand dollars. Now give me my money."

"Not so fast old man, I'll bet my house for your marina." Reaching into his vest pocket, he grabbed the document, put it on the pile of money, and said, "Here is my deed."

Snake yelled excitedly, "It's a deal, show me your hand!"

"Can't do that just yet, how do I know that the marina is worth that much and do you have a clear title with you?"

"Yes, I do and you are just going to have to trust me on the value."

"Did you say that it's at Port Isabell? South Padre Island?"

"Yes," Snake yelled.

"Do you know Eddie Mahan?"

"Yeah, that worthless piece of shit. He crews for the sport-fishing fleet when he feels like it. What does he have to do with this?"

"That worthless piece of shit is my brother and you better hope he confirms you're telling the truth."

Bud looked at the dealer and pointed to the pile of money in the center of the table and said, "Close down this table until I get back from making a phone call. Do not let him go, or touch any money in the pot."

"Okay sir, I'll give you ten minutes."

"Eddie, this is Bud."

"Yeah, Bud. What's up? It's midnight. Do you halve a problem? Is it Marge?"

"Sorry to wake you, but I need your help. How much do you think the marina is worth?"

"Huh? The marina here?"

"Yeah, I think I just won it in a poker game. Is it worth one hundred thousand dollars?"

"It is not very nice, needs a lot of work. But it is the only marina serving the sport-fishing business on South Padre Island. Yeah, just the location is worth one hundred thousand dollars."

"Thanks, Eddie. Go back to sleep."

"Brother, you are one crazy bastard. Tell me about it later. Goodbye."

Bud was back at the table and said, "You got a deal old man. Put your deed out here so I can see it."

Snake slammed the title on the table and was now very agitated. He said, "Stop your crap, show your cards and give me your deed."

By now the table attracted maybe one hundred gamblers looking on and everyone was expecting that Bud was bluffing. They all thought that he had a straight and the old man had a full house. The whole place went wild when he flipped over his hole cards showing the three threes which made his hand a winning four of a kind!

Chapter 2

Bud was on top of the world when he walked through his front door at one in the morning. He was singing and laughing at the top of his lungs.

"Marge, get up. I won! I won big! I want to tell you about it. I'll start the coffee. Come to the kitchen. Come on Marge, get up."

With rollers in her hair and toilet paper plastered around the rollers, she looked like a very pissed-off Indian snake-charmer wearing pajamas and a turban.

Hands on her hips, she sternly said, "You left the file drawer open. I know you took our house deed. You probably didn't even think that it was worthless without both our signatures to make it legal. It's community property, ya know." Not expecting a good response, she held out her hand and said, "Give it back!"

Bud sheepishly reached into his vest pocket and gave both deeds to her.

A pained look came over his face as she looked at the marina deed and after a moment she pointed a finger in his face and said, "This is the last straw. How could you risk our beautiful home at some dumb poker game? We worked years paying this house off, and you risk it all!" Continuing to point, she added, "If you ever do this again, I am gone and out of your life forever. Do you understand? You would be history."

The smile on Bud vanished, as well as the good vibes. He mumbled, "Yeah, you're right. I should have never taken it." He paused a bit and looked up at Marge with his head still hanging down, "I will never do that again."

Marge was still frowning.

He continued but this time with more passion and more volume, "After last night, I am done with gambling. I will never have another thrill as big as that one."

Looking stunned at the unintended insult, she hauled off and hit him right in the chest. Both stopped and looked at each other for a moment, and both burst into laughter ending in a big hug.

"Really," he said, "I played the ultimate poker hand. It cannot get better! I am done."

She picked up the marina deed and read it. "Is this where your brother works in the summer?"

"Yes, I called him last night. He said that the marina does a lot of business with the sport-fishing industry."

Marge forgot all about her anger. After all, they still had the house. Holding the marina title, she said, "I love the ocean. Let's go look at what you just won."

Bud, now smiling again, said, "That's a great idea. I need to talk to an attorney to see if this is valid and can be transferred to us this morning. We can leave tomorrow."

"Sounds exciting, a new chapter in our lives."

"Ya know Marge, I'm sort of tired of West Texas. The ups and downs of the oil business, the hot desert weather, sandstorms, and you have to drive two hours to see a patch of water."

Marge drifted off in thought, "If we like it, we can sell this place and have a nice family business doing something we like, making a nice living, and being happy. I can see that."

By noon, Bud returned to the house. "Marge, the title transfer is done. We are now owners of a marina which we have never even seen." Pausing and laughing, he continued, "We can pop down there tomorrow and check it out. It is only six hundred and fifty miles and takes about twelve hours. It's a piece of cake."

Marge looked at him with a surprised expression, "Well, we better get packing. By the way, Eddie called this morning. I told him a little about it but he wants you to call as soon as you can. He's worried about the fisherman."

Bud finally reached Eddie at the bait shop, "Hi brother, can you believe this?"

"Bud, you have done some wild ass shit in your life but this is the wildest thing you've ever done. What do you know about running a marina?"

"Nothing, but that has never stopped either of us before. Look, I don't want to get into the details, but I actually won it in a big-time Seven Card Stud poker game. I had four threes to beat an ace-high full house."

"Well, you better get your ass down here. The boaters are pretty fickle. If they don't like you, they'll move on."

"We are leaving tomorrow morning. If we don't have any trouble, we should be there day after tomorrow. We'll probably stop at a motel near you and come in after breakfast."

"Just what are you planning to do with this place?"

"Depends Eddie, depends on what we find when we get there. If there is potential, we will sell our house here in Midland and move to the marina. If we don't like what we see, we will sell it."

"Oh, it has tremendous potential but you're not going to like what you see when you get here."

"That bad, huh?"

"You better bring a ton of money to invest in improvements or be willing to work twenty-four hours a day for three years to get it done. That is the bad side."

"Understand, what is the good side?"

"Other than the ocean and the weather, you have the best sport-fishing location in Texas. I'm talking about blue marlin, sailfish, king mackerel, and huge amounts of red fish. Also, the commercial fishing boats are starting to use the marina. Snake was getting four hundred dollars a month for slip rental. If you upgrade the marina, you could get more."

"Now, you're talking my language! How many boats can he park?"

"Bud, you need to get you a book on boating terminology or they will laugh you out of business. You don't park a boat. You should have asked how many slips he has."

"Okay, how many?"

"Right now, I think he can accommodate ten offshore sport-fishing boats and three shrimpers."

Bud busily used his calculator and said, "That is over sixty thousand dollars a year."

"Well yeah, but the bait house brings in another forty thousand dollars, but you have the cost associated with each of those."

"If we add more slips and make some improvements will we get more boats?"

"Once the word gets out you will be covered up."

Bud thought a minute and asked, "How much help did Snake need to run the marina?"

"That was one of the problems. Snake was a cheapskate. He could never keep help and it was a source of continuing bitching from the boat captains. You will need a couple of guys to attend to the boats and fuel lines."

"How about you? Can I count on you to help me run it?"

"Sure, I will help you get started. But you know me, I don't like to be tied down. I need my freedom and I still want to spend the winters in the snow."

"That's okay. Your help during the transition will certainly be appreciated. Oh, a couple of more things. First, be sure Snake gets his items out ASAP. If he is not out by the time I get down there, we will put them in storage. Secondly, tell the boat owners the truth, that I won the marina in a poker game. I suppose that most of those guys gamble every day on fishing and would find it amusing. Tell 'em that I want to meet them in a couple of days."

"Will do. See ya then."

"Looking forward to it. Goodbye."

Chapter 3

"Get up Marge, it's time to go see our marina."

"Okay, I am wide awake. I have been up for an hour just thinking about it."

"Pack your bags, we'll get some coffee and donuts on the way,"

Sharing the drive time, they drove ten hours straight except for fuel, food, and bathroom breaks. They found a nice motel just outside of Brownsville, had dinner at Denny's, and an early night. Tomorrow would be a big day.

They left Brownsville a little after eight, but they took a quick detour to look at the Rio Grande. Marge mentioned that it was the closest large town and how convenient it would be for shopping. Fifteen miles later, they were on the high bridge connecting the mainland to South Padre Island and Port Isabel. With their noses stuck to the windshield, they could not see a single sign of a marina. Soon the road ended and teed off in either direction. If they had continued heading east, they would have been in the Gulf of Mexico.

"Eddie said to take a right and follow it down for about a mile, the marina will be on the right. That doesn't seem correct though, I expected it to face east."

Marge excitedly began pointing, "There it is Bud! Look at the shrimp boats."

Her first impression while approaching the parking lot is that it reminded Marge of pulling into a truck stop on a lonely road in West Texas, underwhelming! Nothing but a rundown metal building and instead of parked trucks, she saw parked boats.

"Well, Eddie said it was not much to look at."

"Look over there," Marge said, pointing to a small mobile home sitting on cinder blocks. "That looks like Eddie walking this way."

"It is. I guess we're here."

After a few hugs, Bud said, "I thought it would face east to the ocean."

Eddie answered his brother's curiosity, "That is actually a good thing. If we get a bad storm or hurricane coming this way the marina and the boats are more protected around here."

"Sure, that's logical."

"What makes this location even better is the very short trip to get out to the Gulf and start fishing. It saves the fishermen tons on fuel money and the fishermen get more time with a hook in the water."

Marge looked around and said, "Not many cars in the parking lot."

"This is still the slow season and it's a weekday. A lot of the fishermen fly private aircraft to fish the weekend."

"That seems expensive just to go catch a fish."

"You will not believe the amount of money these guys spend on a week-end. Saltwater sport-fishing is big money."

Bud was still looking at the surroundings and asked, "Did Snake come and pick up his stuff?"

"Yeah, he didn't have much. He's a single guy and still pissed off at you. He just cleaned out the cash register, hooked up his trailer, and left. Didn't even say goodbye."

"The cash and the mobile home were his, not part of the deal."

"He was not happy."

"Yeah, I'll bet. I stung Snake pretty good."

"Let's get to it. I'll show you around."

Eddie said, "I guess we will start at the office. Like the rest of the marina, it is not much to look at."

Marge announced, "I brought my clipboard. I'll take notes, organize 'em, and print them out when we get back to Midland."

As they rounded the corner of the metal building, both Marge and Dub said, "Ugh, what's that smell?"

Eddie answered, "You will get used to it. It is a combination of the shrimp boats cleaning their nets, washing off their decks, and all the dead fish stink.

Add that to the smell of the sportsman cleaning their catch of the day at the fish cleaning tables and the smell of spilled diesel on the fuel docks. The most offensive smell of all is the raw sewage being dumped out of each boat and into the marina water."

"Why would they do that?"

"Several reasons and Snake is to blame for all of them. He just didn't care."

"Why?"

"The shrimpers are just taking the easiest fastest way to clean the nets. Snake was afraid if he insisted that they clean their nets in the bay they would find another place to dock their boats. Solving the fish-cleaning smell would be easy, just take a little money to move it out to the edge. Each fishing boat has a small service boat called a dinghy, used to hall people or supplies from boat to boat. If you move the fish-cleaning station to the edge of the marina, it may be a little inconvenient for the fishermen but the smell would go away. The fuel dock is a matter of safety. You will need to invest in the latest no-leak nozzle."

Marge was making an ugly face and asked, "How can you fix the sewage?"

That would also take a little money. The marina does not offer a shower or bathrooms and we don't have a pump-out station. The only option now is just to let it flush while it's in the slip. By the way, most upscale marinas have connections to the city utilities and furnish showers and bathrooms."

"Did you get all that Marge?"

"Yep, I think we just spent some more money."

Eddie opened the door to the office and stepped into a large vacant room. It had a desk and a cash register near the front. Scattered about were some tables with chairs, and the tables had either dominoes or playing cards stacked on them. In the back was an old cook stove that hadn't been cleaned since it was new, and a well-used coffee pot on one of the burners.

"What do the fishermen do for meals," asked Marge?

"Brown bag it, or do without," was the reply.

Bud pointed, "What is behind that door?"

As they walked into cold air, Eddie informed them that it was the bait section of the building.

"This is the one thing that the old man did pretty well. There is good money in supplying bait and they must be kept alive. He spent a lot of time here cleaning and keeping the aerator and bubble systems running. He had a deal with the shrimpers. He would buy small mullet and shad they caught along with the shrimp. He also had a bait dealer come by weekly. I think he made as much money from the bait as he did with the slips. If you don't have good access to bait, the fishing boats will go elsewhere."

"Great info Eddie. Let's walk the decks and maybe meet some of the captains."

Bud talked to each boat owner or captain and introduced himself and Marge. Most of them already knew Eddie. Each was concerned that the marina would not stay open. Some expressed opinions on needed changes, repairs, or just wishful thinking. Bud would always end the conversation by honestly informing them of what they could expect.

"Sir, I am here on a fact-finding tour to help evaluate my options. I like the potential here but it will take a lot of time and money to make the changes we think are necessary. It is going to take a few days but I will be back in two weeks to let you know my decision. I will choose between taking on the changes myself or selling it to another marina operator. Either way, this place will get a major overhaul. Thank you for your time."

On the return trip to Midland, Bud and Marge had a constant conversation about the pluses and minuses. Toward the end of the drive, they became more positive and even excited about the opportunity. Each listed what was needed and ranked their ideas as a must-do and then expressed what their dreams could be in the future.

Setting at a truck stop, having a hamburger, Bud said, "I believe that we both want to do this but we don't have enough experience to see the realistic options or dangers. I am not interested in owning a rundown bait shop and a bunch of rickety, rotting old boat docks. I want something we can be proud of and not be forced to work ourselves to death. Hell, look at the ski industry. When Eddie started working ski resorts, Vail was just a tiny town in the mountains with one ski lift. Look at it now, it has become one of the premier ski resorts in the world. Make it nice and the money will flow. The more exotic the sport, the more the rich will want to come. Vail must be worth billions now."

"You don't think we can do that, do you?"

"No, but we can make more than we can ever spend."

"You have always been a dreamer. What do you want to do?

"I want to fly to Miami. They have hundreds of upscale marinas serving the sport-fishing and yachting markets. I want to get some ideas. Maybe even meet someone who wants to buy the marina. While I am gone, I want you to find a realtor and get an estimate of what we can expect if we sell our home. When I come back, we should have the information to make a good decision."

"Okay Marge, it has been ten days since we were on South Padre Island. We know what I've found out in Florida, and we know we should get one hundred and ten thousand dollars for our house. Are you ready to make a decision?"

"I am both worried and excited, but we will never get this opportunity again. Let's do it."

Bud responded, "I agree, but we need one more piece of the puzzle."

"What?"

"A plan. In business, it is called a five-year plan. We can't get it all done at once. The plan will be something that we can give to the people down there so that they will have an idea what to expect."

"Where do we start?"

"I've been giving it some thought. Here's what I have as a beginning." He handed a bunch of papers to Marge and said, "Maybe you can make this look a little more professional."

She looked at it and began to read out loud.

"'The Swordfish Marina.' Say, I like the new name."

"Leave the side comments for a while, just read."

"Year one:

- Buy a camper. (Not part of the plan, but we have to stay somewhere)
- Build a sizeable shaded community dock with tables, chairs, vending machines, restrooms, and showers
- Improve the fuel dock to become part of the community dock
- Replace and move the fish cleaning table to the end of the marina
- Remodel the central area to include a small office. The more substantial space will consist of a small kitchen and tables and chairs. To start, we will serve food only on Saturday and Sunday.
- Proposed new rules that would include no dumping of raw sewage or

trash in the marina. If you don't have a holding tank, use the new community facilities. Failure to comply with this will forfeit your rental contract and you must move out of the marina. Commercial fisherman must clean nets and gear before entering the marina.

Year two:

- Begin dock expansion.
- Docks will be constructed using the new floating design made of steel, concrete decking, and floatation. The docks will be attached to sizeable thirty-foot steel poles driven down into the mud at least ten feet. Stabilization will be steel cross members connected to each pole underwater. The design will allow for the ups and downs of tides and even accommodate a storm surges of ten or fifteen feet. This construction is similar to those found in the upscale Florida marinas.
- Power and water will be available for each slip.
- We will build one dock line per year. The docks can accommodate seven slips on either side for a total of fourteen slips.
- Existing customers have the right to move to the new slips at no extra charge.
- Continue expanding food service by using Mexican cooks and laborers.

Year three to five:

- Continue on this schedule each year.
- In the end, it should accommodate approximately seventy sport and commercial fishing boats."

"Marge, if we can keep to this plan, we should bring in about half a million per year. Of course that is gross profits but still that would bring a lot of money to us, more than we've ever dreamed of having."

"Sounds too easy. What do you know about construction?"

"I forgot to tell you, Eddie has agreed to supervise the construction. He is a great welder and can save a lot of money by doing that himself. Of course,

I will pay him his usual rates. That means that we would only do construction during the summer months, but that's okay as we will be on a tight budget and can't overspend our money. We have to make money from the existing slips all year to build up the cash account. Then we would have the funds to build in the summers. Okay Marge, are you in or out?"

"I am all in."

"Now Marge, that sounds a lot like a gambling term."

"I know, I feel the thrill. Baby, let's roll the dice."

The meeting with the boat owners and captains went well. Marge had the plan printed and gave each owner or captain a copy as they filed into the open office. She had even had one posted on the window of the door. Everyone seemed to like what Bud had envisioned and none expressed any objections to the new rules. Bud thanked everyone for coming and as the last one exited, Marge reached in the ice chest and pulled three cold beers.

I will pay you in the spring. I [illegible] could only [illegible] during the summer months [illegible] and [illegible] camp [illegible] open I can manage. We [illegible] all year to build up the cash account [illegible] would [illegible] in the autumn. Okay, Marge, [illegible]?"

"[illegible]"

"Now Marge, that sounds [illegible]"

[illegible] the thrill [illegible]

[illegible] meeting with the [illegible]

[illegible] planned and [illegible] each owner [illegible]

office. [illegible] had even had [illegible]

[illegible] had [illegible]

the [illegible]. [illegible] [illegible]

[illegible] the [illegible] and [illegible]

Chapter 4

The spring of 1963, a Dallas T.V. station began a weekly people-of-interest program as the lead-in to the CBS Evening News with Walter Cronkite. It featured a sparkling new face, Jill Wilkerson, interviewing various famous people located throughout Texas. It was called Texas Legends and Characters. They were typically looking for renowned sports heroes, professional football and baseball owners, oilmen, politicians, bankers, or even astronauts. The producers had the idea of finding the most extreme example of the Texas gambler. Asking around, they kept hearing about this Midland man who won a Gulf Coast marina serving the Texas sport-fishing industry.

It did not take long to track down Bud Mahan. A producer made the appointment and the entire crew was excited. A truck was loaded with gear and they began the two-day drive. The producers and Jill Wilkerson flew into Brownsville and rented a car.

That afternoon, Bud welcomed the T.V. crew while the equipment was being set up on the large, shaded community dock. The make-up girls were busy with Jill and even spent a little time on Bud. The plan was to shoot a lot of footage and edit it into a thirty-minute segment when they returned to Dallas. The first interview began with Bud and Jill sitting at a table with the fishing boats in the background.

They filmed the introductions and Jill began the interview.

"This is gorgeous and clean, smells just like the ocean. Tell me about it."

"Well, it sure didn't start out this way. It was pretty bad when we saw it for the first time. That was back in 1958. It was old, broken-down, and smelly. Most everything you see now is new. Our five-year renovation plan is almost complete."

"What else are you going to do?"

"Eventually, we will double but right now we are at sort of a halt in construction. I don't want to extend ourselves during this recession."

"Have you been hurt by the recession?"

"Not too much. You see we service the entertainment market for the idle rich. I compare us to the high-dollar ski resorts like Vail. It has to be a lot worse than this for our customers to start selling their fishing boats. They must have a place to keep them and we are one of the cheapest marinas in the whole U.S. Plus we have great fishing, second to none!"

"You are using the word 'we', do you have a partner?"

"Not an investment partner. It's my life partner and wife, Marge."

"Oh, will I get to meet her?"

"I have no idea. She has her own schedule."

"Did you always have an interest in boats and a marina?"

"Absolutely not. I grew up in West Texas and I only saw the ocean two times before I came down here. The only time I thought about owning a marina was that memorable poker night in 1958."

"Well, you have transitioned right into the subject I am here to discuss. The rumor has it that you actually won this playing poker. Is that correct?"

"Yes."

"How? Tell me about it."

"We weren't purposely playing for the marina. It was at a multi-table poker game in Midland. Must have had seventy players from all over. We were playing Seven Card Stud. My opponent had a full house and placed a large bet. Unbeknownst to him, I had four threes." Pausing, he asked Jill, "You do know that four threes will beat a full house?"

"Yes, then what happened?"

"That was the best poker hand I have ever played. Earlier, my opponent had mentioned that he owned a marina. So, as everyone was watching for my response. Not only did I accept the bet, I raised it, stating that I would bet my Midland home for his marina."

"You did what?"

"Yeah, I ask him if his marina was worth one hundred thousand dollars and he said it was. I made him prove it. All along he still believed that his full house was an easy winner and he accepted. You should have seen his face when I turned over my hand and he saw the four threes."

"Wow, you must have nerves of steel."

"Oh, I was pretty stressed but tried not to show it."

"What a story! Do you still gamble?"

"I would say that selling my perfectly good home in Midland and moving down here was a pretty big gamble."

"Yeah, but that was a business decision. I mean, do you still play big-time poker?"

"No, Marge nearly killed me when she found out that I bet the house. I made her a promise, never again. However, we do have a Wednesday poker night here with a one dollar ante and a five dollar limit on bets. Friendly game. We have a mayor, two sheriffs, a banker, and a couple of local ranchers. We all enjoy it and go home at ten."

"Just play poker?"

"No, mostly laugh, drink, and discuss whatever is on their minds at the time. Subjects could be anything, but are sure to include fishing, hunting, politics, and women."

"Do you get bored?"

"Not really, I get all the excitement I need right here."

"Well, that about completes the interview. How about a tour?"

The group walked the decks and interviewed a few captains. One even invited them to come aboard his boat. He was very proud of the eighty-foot sport-fishing boat. He said that it was worth more than a million and a half dollars. At the end of the pier, they also looked at a couple of shrimp boats. As they meandered back to the main building, they could smell a pot of gumbo cooking.

"Stay for a while and have lunch with us," Bud offered.

"Thanks but no thanks. We all have a schedule to make. Our flight leaves in two hours."

As the crew was packing the equipment, Jill was looking at the giant trophies of blue marlin and sailfish mounted on the walls when Marge came in with a big smile on her face. She was carrying a little baby boy.

"Look everyone. Meet our new nephew, Jack Mahan."

Part Two - Freedom

Chapter 5

My mother was a hippie and my father was an adrenaline junkie. Other than that, I was mostly normal. I was born in a motel somewhere on the way to South Padre Island, where my father was working summers at the Swordfish, and I guess my mom was just tagging along for a little time on the beach. But there I was, nine-pounds three-ounces and blue eyes. I don't even know if I have a birth certificate but if I did, it would read "Jack Mahan, boy, born on April 18, 1963 - Howard County, Texas".

Folks called my father a risk taker, daredevil, or thrill seeker. The truth is that he was an excellent father, but he would do almost anything for the rush of adrenaline and he had the scars to prove it. If he had a résumé it would list skydiving, scuba diving, mountain climbing, kayak racing, cave exploring, bear wrestling, ski instructor, and an attempt to set the motorcycle world speed record at the Bonneville Salt Flats. He could never turn down a chance to experience a thrill.

My mom, on the other hand, was a true flower child. She was possessed with the Vietnam War and was always marching in protest. When I was just four, she hitchhiked to Washington D.C. to attend a massive rally and demonstration. She never came back.

Dad would follow his heart and as we traveled I was always riding shotgun. We spent summers on South Padre Island at Uncle Bud's marina. It was very isolated and out of main-stream tourist activity. The fishing was excellent and the beaches practically deserted. There he worked as the Construction Foreman managing the build-out of the Swordfish expansion program.

Later on, as the dock expansion slowed down, we had saved enough money for us to build a beach house. We located it on the ocean side of the island about three hundred yards east of the marina. From there we had an unobstructed view of the beach, surf, and the Gulf of Mexico. By then I was ten and we worked together as a team. It wasn't much to look at but it was very functional. We built the cabin on sawed-off telephone poles and buried them ten feet deep in the sand. The frame and roof were double-supported to help it survive a small hurricane. We had two bedrooms and a combination kitchen and living area. Of course it was air-conditioned. The beautiful thing was that we paid cash as we built which mean no debt, the title was free and clear.

When we finished, we looked around with pride. It was less than two miles to Port Isabel and just a stone's throw to the marina, but right outside were the unspoiled white sands of South Padre Island. The government did not open the island to the public until 1962. Dad was one of the first to buy a small piece of paradise. We had access to over fifty miles of beach to explore and most of the time did not see a single human being the whole day.

At the end of August we would pack the pickup and head north to Colorado. To be exact, it was Vail. There my dad had a full-time job working the ski lifts and giving beginner lessons to the tourists. The pay was good plus we were given room and board at the lodge. The town of Vail was large enough to have a public school system and it was there where I attended first through the eleventh grade. I was a better than average student but not near the top of the class.

During his idle time, Dad was either mountain climbing or downhill racing with the ski club. Most of the time he would show up to work the next day without a single broken bone.

At the end of the school year, we would pack up and drive back to the beach. It was here, just before my senior year, that Dad got the call. I knew it was serious as he talked on the phone for hours at a time and afterward he would stay awake most nights.

I woke up that Saturday morning and my dad was busy cooking. This activity was unusual as he never ate breakfast. He was an emotional wreck.

He sat down with me and said, "Jack, please forgive me for what I am about to tell you."

Thinking that he was going to join his friends on a two-day adventure to search for gold, I said, "Okay Dad, I can handle it."

"Son, I have the opportunity of a lifetime. If I don't take it, I may never have the chance to do it again."

"Okay, what is it?"

"A buddy of mine in California has just bought a sailboat. He wants me to help crew while we sail around the world."

"Wow."

"I will be gone maybe two or three years."

I just stared.

"I have to go Jack. I will never have this chance again."

"Can I go?" I ask.

"No, too many dangers and you must finish school."

"You want me to go back to Vail?"

"No, you will stay here in the beach house to finish high school. I am sorry, but you can handle it. You have been taking care of yourself for years. I know you are ready to fend for yourself."

He went on to tell me that he was giving me the house and half his savings.

He said, "I gave the deed and a check for fifteen thousand dollars to Uncle Bud at the marina. You can pick it up anytime. I must leave soon, need to be in San Diego in two days. I will try to keep in touch."

I was in shock. However, after thinking about it, I knew that he had to chase one more major adventure before settling down. I loved him and I had to let him go. After all, I felt a strange tinge of jealousy. I watched him pack very little gear or clothes. I guess he didn't need it on the boat. He left me all his tools, welding machine, scuba gear, and a generator. He was both sad and happy as he pulled onto the road and waved goodbye. I continued to watch until he disappeared into the distance. Then I went back inside and cried.

The next day was the start of my new life. The reality of taking care of myself was a little scary. I sat down and made a list of what I should do for the next two weeks. School was not on that list. I walked over to the Sailfish, where Uncle Bud was waiting for me.

I had known Bud and Marge Mahan almost from the day I was born. I affectionately called him just by his first name or Uncle Bud. When I asked him about the money, his response utterly destroyed my list.

"I made a promise to your dad and I always keep my promises. He wants you to finish high school first. Then you may do whatever you wish with it."

"How am I going to eat or pay expenses while I go to school?"

"You can work here at the bait house part time and I can get you on the standby list as a deck-hand for the fishing fleet."

"How am I going to get to school?"

"You can walk or take the bus, but you can also take a correspondence course and finish school by taking a test. You pass and you graduate."

"Will it take long?"

"You may finish as slow or as fast as you wish."

"Thanks, Uncle Bud. I'll pick up my check in a month."

It took me six weeks to finish the course and pass the test. I officially graduated from public school. Next stop was to get the cash and set up a checking account. Uncle Bud went with me to the bank and helped set up automatic bill payment for the electric company and the city water department along with a savings account. Then we went to his insurance agent to sign up for home, auto, and health insurance, again with payments drafted by the bank. I was all set.

I found a dune buggy listed in the Corpus Christi paper and borrowed Uncle Bud's truck to check it out. The vehicle was in great shape and was street legal. It was not fancy but it was built to take the rigors of the beaches. It had a sturdy tube frame, VW engine, big tires with large treads, and headlights mounted on the roll bar. After a test drive, I gave the man a check for $1,550 and rolled it on the trailer. I closed the truck door, adjusted the mirrors, and excitedly hauled it back to the beach house. There I modified the buggy to fit my needs. I planned to roam the beaches and find items that I could sell.

I welded a metal mesh bed to the frame above the engine, sort of like a pickup bed. Then I added a couple of holders for a trash can and a water jug. A front-mounted hook and a small hand winch finished it out. Now! I am ready to make beachcombing my business.

It didn't take long to learn how to clean seashells and bleach them so they wouldn't smell and were nice and shiny. That process usually took about two weeks but it required very little labor. The easy money was with the timber or driftwood planks I found. When I had a load, I would drive three hours to Corpus Christi and Aransas Pass. Here I would go to the many artists and art collectors to sell my goods. The majority of my income was from the extremely weathered wood which was used for frames or just mounted for display. I would typically bring back two to three hundred dollars per week.

Chapter 6

On one of my daily drives along the beach, I noticed an unusual shape floating just outside the breaking surf, maybe two hundred yards out. I stopped to observe it for a while. I thought it was a wooden container that may have fallen off a cargo ship during a storm. Continuing to watch, I could see it was a large piece of wreckage which was barely floating. Using my binoculars, I determined that it was a capsized wooden lifeboat positioned upside-down. It looked to be about the size of a garage door and something was laying on top.

Just as it was beginning to enter the surf, I made it out to possibly be a dingy black and white dog. Once the wreckage reached the surf, the dog would undoubtedly fall. I swam out to get a closer look and sure enough, it was a dog and it was in horrible shape. Its nose and feet were sunburned and bleeding and it was very sick from drinking the salt water. As I reached up and pulled the dog into the water, I was thankful that I had slipped on my life jacket. Shortly we were on the beach.

I pulled an old shell from the dune buggy and poured in fresh water. The dog's swollen tongue prohibited it from drinking. I held his head up and poured water into his mouth. The hydration helped, but he was frail and needed medical attention. Immediately, we were on our way to Uncle Bud's and then on to a vet.

The vet gave him an IV and antibiotic shots. He told me that I had saved the dog's life. He couldn't have survived much longer. The vet wanted to keep him a couple of days to be sure he didn't have a setback or enter into shock. A few days later, I pulled into the vet's office where I found a tired, but wagging, tail. The vet said that he just needed a lot of rest and nourishment.

I asked, "What kind of dog is it?"

"He appears to be a full-blooded Australian Shepherd. He is not a pup, maybe two years old."

"An Australian Shepherd? There is nothing on the news concerning an Australian flagged shipwreck."

"Oh no. The dog is not from Australia. In fact, I have no idea why it's called an Australian Shepherd because it's a U.S. breed. It is a working dog, mostly used on cattle ranches. They are brilliant and very easy to train. You can see them all the time performing at horse shows and rodeos. They love to work."

"Can I keep him?"

"Yes, but bring him back for a checkup next week and we'll give him his rabies shots to make him legal. What are you going to name him?"

"In honor of his breed, I may call him Blimey."

"Blimey? Where did that come from?"

"I had an Australian friend in high school who always used the word blimey. It is like we use the word wow. Like, 'blimey it's hot out here' or maybe 'blimey that's a nice-looking horse'. I think I will name him Blimey."

It didn't take long for Blimey and me to become bonded like brothers. I thought that if he is a working dog, I had better teach him something useful. Within a week he would bring my tool bag, a hammer, or a forty-foot floating ski rope that I kept rolled up. By the next, he was even putting these items back in the buggy on my command. After that, I began to teach him things that would actually assist me while I was picking up items on the beach. The rope had a loop on one end and the buggy had a hook on the front frame next to the winch. On my command of "hook the rope", he would carry the loop end to the buggy and place the loop over the hook. We used this all the time when I was trying to pull a log out of the sand. He could do other things such as finding a tool which I may have dropped in the surf or the beach. We were a team.

What a life we had. Absolute freedom! Occasionally we would explore up and down the beaches as far as twenty miles and then pitch a tent, start a campfire, and spend a day or two. We would catch fish or crabs and eat like kings. Sometimes I wonder what my classmates were doing, but I knew it couldn't be better than this.

Six months later, Blimey and I were exploring the northern beaches about fifty miles from the cabin. South Padre is a barrier island separating the Texas coast from the Gulf of Mexico. As I traveled up and down the beach, I noticed that sometimes the island is wide and others it's narrow. Rivers emptying into the ocean will erode the beach and cause it to become smaller or sometimes even disappear altogether. Typically, this offers the best wade fishing and that day I was in the mood to fish.

The tide was out and I noticed a pool of water bubbling up very near the inward beach, a perfect spot to wade out and cast a lure. I was barefoot and felt the change in the consistency of the sand. Beaches usually are course and compact as I stand on it. However, this part of the beach was being fed from a river or maybe an underground spring and was very wet and loosely packed. I continued to wade out to get a little closer to where I wanted to fish. Blimey was laying in the shade of the buggy.

Within four more steps, I knew that I was in trouble. My feet started to sink downward, and before I could back out, I was waist deep.

"Oh crap! Quicksand!"

I started to take a step backward but I could not move either leg. The more I struggled, the more I sank. I bent over and put my arms out, but I continued to sink. I tried to relax and think. Blimey sensed trouble and began to bark and run my way. I shouted for him to stay. He did. I now realized that this was low tide and it would rise about three feet in an hour or two. If I didn't get out, I would drown.

What are my options? I could send Blimey back to find Uncle Bud, but even if Blimey makes it to the marina, it is too far. They will never get back in time.

Gripping my fishing rig, I looked down and realized it had strong forty-pound test line on the reel. I cast over to the buggy and hung the lure on the roll bar. Maybe I can crank myself to safety. The rod bent over almost in the shape of a U, but no luck. I then dropped the rod and took the line in my hands. I could feel that I was slowly moving! Suddenly, it snapped and I settled back into the quicksand. Frantically, I extended my hands to retrieve the rod but came up empty. Now I had lost any chance of using the rod and reel for escape.

I remembered the ski rope I had stored in the buggy. I started to call Blimey but realized that when he carried it out to me, he would also sink into the quicksand. I would have to wait until the tide starts to come in enough for Blimey to swim the rope to me. It is my only chance.

The wait was terrifying. Doubts were running through my mind. *Can Blimey retrieve the rope as we practiced? Will he swim back to the buggy and put the loop over the hook? Was it even long enough?*

I was going crazy as I realized that I was out of options. The tide was finally changing and it was coming in quickly. The water is now up to my chest.

I called out, "Blimey, bring me the rope. Bring me the rope, boy!"

He perked up, ran to the buggy, and ran back with the rope coil in his mouth but stopped at water's edge. The image of the shipwreck was still in his mind and he did not want to go in the water.

I called again and his ears pointed back as he splashed into the water and began swimming to me with the rope in his mouth.

Okay, the next step is the hardest, I thought.

I took the rope, untied the coil, and gave Blimey the loop end.

"Hook the rope, Blimey. Hook the rope!" and pointed to the buggy. I watched with delight to see him swim off towards the hook dragging the floating rope.

By now the water was up to my mouth. I could only see Blimey between waves. He was almost there.

Blimey began to bark excitedly and I hoped he had enough rope to get back to the buggy. A gentle pull on the line felt secure. A more substantial test and the rope tightened. He did it! I began to pull with all my might. Five minutes later, I was laying on the beach with Blimey licking my face. I was alive!

I rested there few minutes, then went over to the gulf side of the island where I waded out to wash off the mud. Back on the beach, I just sat there with Blimey at my side and tried settling down to let my heart rate get back to normal.

I looked over at him and said, "Thank you, we are now even."

He gave me a bark.

Later that night back at the beach house, I whispered to no one in particular, "I now know what makes Dad tick. The adrenaline rush was the most powerful experience of my life, but I *do not* want to do that again!"

Part Three –

An Unexpected Friendship

Chapter 7

Deputy Sherriff Thompson was on his routine morning rounds when he pulled his cruiser off the road and onto the beach. The sun had been up nearly an hour and as the tide moved out the seagulls were scavenging scraps at the water's edge. He could also see a lone hiker aimlessly walking in the wet sand.

It was his favorite time of the day. He rolled the windows down, turned off the engine, and kept the police radio at its lowest volume, allowing him to hear the sounds of the ocean. Reaching over for the sack, he opened his morning coffee and took the first bite of the glazed donut. He thought that it could not be any better. Before his second bite, his peaceful day ended when an All-Points Bulletin blasted over the radio.

"Armed robbery reported at the convenience store on Ocean Drive and forty eighth Street. Shots fired, clerk down. EMS dispatched. The suspect left the store on foot. Be on the lookout for a young male in dark clothing with a hoodie, carrying a backpack. Consider him armed and dangerous."

Officer Thompson said to himself, "Jesus, that's not two miles from here!"

He grabbed his binoculars and looked at the person on the beach. Focusing in, he saw that he was wearing a black hoodie and had a backpack. Trying to keep his adrenaline in check, he radioed in that he had a suspicious person walking the beach and that he would approach.

At this time, the hiker had not noticed the police cruiser. Thompson started the vehicle and eased down the beach. Hearing the crushing of seashells, the hiker turned to look as the officer turned on the flashers and pulled closer. The hiker did not seem alarmed, nor did he try to escape.

Thompson stepped out of the car, pointed his pistol, and shouted, "Hands up and you will not get hurt!"

He then noticed that this was one of the largest men he had ever seen. He thought, *this guy must be seven feet tall.*

The hiker asked, "What do you want officer?"

Thompson said, "Just get down on your knees, and keep your hands high."

"But I didn't do anything wrong."

"Just precautions. Do as I say until I get you checked out. If you are okay, I will let you go."

"How long will this take?"

"Not long. Now, I must cuff you, but first you need to toss me the backpack."

"You will find a gun in there. It's not loaded. I don't even know if it works. But here it is," as the boy lobbed it to the deputy.

He picked up the backpack and pitched handcuffs to the giant and said, "Put these cuffs on. I have a backup on the way and it will be much easier if you do this yourself."

The hiker complied and Thompson asked if he had any ID.

"Yeah, my driver's license is in my wallet. It's in my back pocket."

Thompson fished out the card, "Says here you are Hector Gomez and you are six-foot-five and weigh two hundred and fifty-five pounds. That correct?"

"Yeah. I may have gained a few pounds since I got the license."

As the officer was putting him in the secure back seat, Hector asked, "Just what do you think I did?"

"Armed robbery and by the way, thanks for cooperating with me. I will note that in the write-up."

The officer grabbed the backpack and lifted it to the hood of the cruiser.

"Mind if I take a look in your backpack?"

"No, I have already told you there is a gun in there. By the way, that is all the money I have, don't lose it."

At this time, other squad cars came rolling up.

"Need any help Thompson?"

"Not now, see you guys back at the office."

Chapter 8

Officer Thompson arrived at the station amidst what seemed to be every cop in the county. They all followed Hector in and escorted him to the booking desk.

"What do we have here Deputy?" the Sergeant asked.

Everyone was shocked to hear his answer, "I am not sure Sergeant. Looks like he could be our man, but just as easily he could be an innocent bystander. Can we not book him but just hold him for a few hours until we get some more facts?"

"You're getting soft, aren't you Deputy?"

"Just give me a little time. Let me talk to the D.A."

"Okay, but it will be up to the D.A. Don't be disappointed, he is getting to be a real hard-ass."

"Yeah, I know. Thanks Sarge."

"Put him in the secure interview room, the one behind the locked bars. Keep the cuffs on him and you will not talk to him until the D.A. shows up."

Hector looked at Thompson, smiled a little, and said, "Thanks."

Right before lunch, Thompson received a call from Detective Adam Carlson to meet him at the station at 11:30.

"I'll bring some fried chicken for three. The convenience store clerk did not die and is talking now. Should have an ID soon. The D.A. wants some movement on your boy soon. Still, have no other leads on the robbery and he wants to book Hector early enough to get it in tonight's paper."

"Okay, but I want to review the case before we talk to him. See you then."

They gave one serving to Hector and ate the rest in a private conference room.

Detective Carlson said, "I had no idea Hector was this big. That is one point in his favor, as the witness ID'ed the attacker as average height and weight. Did you see the surveillance tape?"

"No, it was out of order, but here is the backpack. You will find a gun in there. Take a look at it."

Pulling the gun out of the backpack, the detective said, "A .38 revolver. It looks like it hasn't been cleaned in years and it doesn't smell like it was fired this morning." Looking up the detective said, "This gun is not the one that was used. Of course, Hector could have ditched the real gun to create a denial. Other than that, he does not have an alibi."

"Another point in his favor is the total cash in his backpack is forty-seven dollars."

"Yeah, I noticed. Where's the money from the robbery?"

"Yes and the kid had no idea why I was cuffing him. He never tried to escape or become aggressive. He has cooperated the entire way. I will bet he could pass a lie detector."

"I know, but the D.A. is not going to let him free on your feelings."

"Well, let's go talk to him."

"Can't do that. I have to talk to Hector alone."

Five minutes later, Hector and Detective Carlson were facing each other across a small table. For safety reasons, and considering his size, the cuffs remained securely around his wrists.

"Hello Hector, my name is Detective Carlson but you can call me Adam if you like."

"I prefer just to call you Detective and thank you for the chicken."

"Yeah, I'll bet a guy your size could get hungry in a hurry."

"Sometimes, but I had a great meal last night and breakfast this morning with a new friend of mine."

"Interesting, but I would like to start from the beginning. Where did you grow up? Your driver's license lists an address in Corpus Christi. We checked and found out that it's a foster home. They had nice things to say about you."

"Yes, I have been with them for six years. But you must keep them out of the news. They may be in danger."

"Danger? How? Hector are you in a gang?

"No, I hate gangs. But that is the problem."

"I don't understand. How about you start from the beginning."

"Okay Detective, but it's a long story."

"I have a couple of hours. Let's hear it."

"I was born in Galveston in 1964. My father lost his life in the Vietnam War and my mom raised my brother and me the best she could.

"Sorry to hear about your dad."

"You haven't heard the worst of it yet."

"Go on, I am listing."

"My brother was older and was on the football team at Galveston High School. Popular, nice guy, but got involved with drugs. Not the hard stuff, mostly weed. Started selling it to the team for fun. Got behind on his payments to the gang and they became pissed. They threatened him a lot. He finally told them that he wanted out. His coaches were asking questions."

"That sounds reasonable. It happens a lot. Continue."

"He sold his car to make the payment, but the gang still was not happy."

"They were afraid he would turn them in?"

"Yeah, that's it. Anyway, Mom was picking him up from football practice and as they were pulling away from the school, the gang did a drive-by shooting. Killed him and my mom."

"Where were you?"

"In the car, but I was laying down in the back seat. They did not see me, but I saw everything."

"That is awful! How old were you?"

"Eight."

"What happened then?"

"Child Protective Services placed me in foster care in Galveston, but soon the courts moved me to Corpus to get me out of the danger of the gang."

"Okay, continue."

They set me up with the Philip family. Friendly people, especially Mrs. Philip. I eventually began calling her 'Mom'. That is when I started to grow. I got my size from my dad and my aunt thinks that I will even be bigger."

"What happened there to cause you to run away?"

"I am a senior and ready to graduate. Wanted to go to tech school to learn diesel mechanics. Wanted to work on boats. Ya' know, here in Corpus. The gang found me again. I don't know if it was the same leader, but it was the same gang, the El Lobos. They think they're real bad-asses. They wouldn't leave me alone. Yesterday, they saw me walking to school and they grabbed me and took me to a remote beach near Aransas Pass.

"How many were in the car?"

"Three plus me. As we stood on the beach, the boss man asked if I once lived in Galveston. Said they knew of a Hector Gomez there. I knew that if I told them, they would kill me and my foster family. I couldn't let that happen. They each had a gun tucked into the front of their pants and they were taking turns pushing me. When it was the leader's turn, I grabbed his arm and broke it over my knee. I took his gun and dropped it, I then turned him around and put him in a bear hug. He was kicking and screaming."

"Go on."

"The other two drew their guns, but I told them to drop them or I would break his neck. The boss man shouted for them to drop the guns and they did. I told them to back away and get in the car. That is when the anger hit me. I thought about my mom and my brother. I couldn't help myself. I started squeezing as hard as I could. I heard several ribs crack and he started making funny noises as he tried to catch his breath. Maybe punctured his lungs. Then I just lifted him up over my head and threw him onto the hard beach road. Think I may have killed him."

"We will check the hospitals, but go on."

"I grabbed his gun and pointed it at the other two. I picked up their guns and told them to get out of my sight and take this *slimeball* with you. After they were gone, I threw the guns in the ocean and walked back home. I knew it did not matter if I killed that S.O.B. or not, I was a dead man and so was my foster family. I packed my backpack and left a note that I was going away and not to report it to anyone."

"Okay, how did you get back to the beach and what happened last night and this morning?"

"I thought that I must avoid the highways because they would be looking for me, so I walked to the beach and turned right. Sometime around five or six, a dune buggy came rolling to a stop and this slim guy said hello. He had the buggy fixed up real nice. Also had a dog riding shotgun. His name was Jack and his dog was called Blimey."

"What was he doing there?"

"He was a beachcomber, picks up shells and driftwood and sells it to the art community. Said he had an uncle that has a marina down at the tip of Texas. He was on his way back after selling his stuff. Wanted to catch some flounder to take back to his uncle. Didn't ask many questions, but offered me twenty bucks to help him spear some flounders and he would also cook some for our supper."

'Did you catch any?"

"Yeah, about ten or fifteen. We cleaned the fish and put all but three in his ice chest. Cooked the three on the fire we had that night."

"Why didn't the deputy see him this morning?"

"I guess he just missed him. Jack got up early to put some more ice in his chest and then he had about a three-hour drive home."

Turning off the recorder, Detective Carlson stood.

"That's enough for right now Hector. I need some time to check out your story. Just sit tight here and I will be back as soon as possible. By the way, I have two more questions."

"Okay Detective, ask away."

"First, where did you get the gun you had in your backpack?

"Jack gave it to me, said he found it last week on a beach. Said it wouldn't work, but it may scare a bad character away. What is the other question?"

"I need to contact Jack. Do you have his number?"

"I don't even know his last name but his uncle owns a marina on South Padre Island at the southern tip of Texas near Port Isabel. He called him Uncle Bud. You may find him there."

"I'll be back as soon as possible. Maybe I can get those cuffs off."

Chapter 9

Detective Carlson called a meeting with Officer Thompson to discuss what he had discovered. While he was waiting for the officer, he asked the Desk Sergeant to remove the cuffs but to keep Hector in the locked interrogation room.

In less than ten minutes, the officer was at the station and talking to the detective.

"You know Thompson, I think you were correct. I don't believe that he had anything to do with the convenience store robbery, but to get his release we need to cover our ass. As I see it, we will need to do the following. I want you to go the hospital and get a detailed statement from the store clerk. Take a photo of Hector but don't show it to him until he describes his assailant. Then get confirmation that Hector was or was not the one that shot him.

"While you are at the hospital, see if they had an emergency room visit from a young man that had a broken wrist and cracked ribs. If he is still there, get a statement of the accident and ask about the robbery. I will see if I can find the mystery lad with a dune buggy and the uncle who owns a marina in South Padre. If I can find him, I will need to have him come back for a statement. Let's get this done before your shift changes. If we don't get it wrapped up by five o'clock, I'll have to book the boy and he'll spend the night in jail."

"Yes sir, I'm on my way."

A call to the police department at Port Isabel was successful in getting the phone number of the only marina within fifty miles. They even got the name of the owner, Mr. Bud Mahan.

Mr. Mahan confirmed that his nephew, Jack, dropped by that morning and gave him some fresh flounder. He added that Jack and a young man had caught the fish the night before, but could not remember his name.

Detective Carlson said, “A young man was picked up this morning on the beach and hauled in on suspicion of robbing a convenience store. This young man claims that he was with Jack when the robbery occurred.”

Mr. Mahan responded, “That is a serious accusation. How can I help?”

“We don’t believe he did it, but we need some credible facts to let him go. Can you get Jack to come back to Corpus to make a statement? If not, we will have to book this man and he will spend a night in Jail.

“Thanks for the information detective, we’ll leave shortly and should be there by five o’clock.”

“Thank you, Mr. Mahan.”

Officer Thompson arrived back at the station at four and found the detective at a table talking to other officers. He said, “Hey, glad you’re back. What did you find?”

“A lot sir,” as he grabbed a chair and sat down at the table. “Nothing from the store camera, hasn’t worked for weeks. Why do they even have one? But, the clerk confirmed that the thief was no taller than six-foot and was thin. Showed him the picture and he said it was not him.”

“We already expected that. What else ya have?”

“Our gangbanger was brought in to the emergency room yesterday afternoon. Severely broken hand, may not ever use it again, and multiple broken ribs and a punctured lung.”

“That jives with what Hector told me.”

“Wait, there is more. He paid with a credit card with the name of Jerry Jackson. Later it came up stolen but by that time the thugs had checked out.”

“Model citizens on display,” laughed the Detective.

“One more thing. The nurses overheard that they were planning to find Hector and kill him and whoever is with him.”

“Thanks Officer, stick around for a while. The folks from the marina will be here within the hour. Let’s see what they have to say.”

“By the way, we still don’t know the thug’s name but we now know for sure he is in a gang.”

"Really?"

"Nurses said they each had a wolf's head tattooed on their wrist."

"The El Lobos, they are making a move to control the narcotics trade along the Texas Coast, real bad reputation."

It was a little before five when Bud and Jack pulled into the station parking lot. Both Officer Thompson and Detective Carlson were waiting in the conference room. Hector was still in the holding room however the officer told him that Jack was on his way.

After the introduction, the detective started with the inquiry.

"Jack, may I call you Jack?"

"Sure."

"Tell me, in your own words, when you first met Hector Gomez."

"I am a professional beachcomber. I find shells and weathered lumber and sell them to the tourist shops and the local artist. I had just delivered a load to my Aransas Pass art contacts and took a long way home. You know, looking for sellable stuff on the beach. I had already told Uncle Bud that I would spend the night and bring back some fish: The best time to flounder fish is at night. I knew a good shallow place just south of Corpus, that's where I was going to stay."

The detective asked, "About what time was that?"

"Sun was still up. I'd guess about eight. When my dog started barking, he's my constant companion, I looked around and saw this giant strolling toward me. I was still in my dune buggy and, not knowing what I was about to get into, I reached for my gun and put it in my lap.

"Well, this giant of a guy turned out to be the friendliest fellow ever! I asked him why he was alone walking the beach and he said that he had a run-in with some gang members. Said he was running away and hiding. I asked him where he lived and he said that he had just left his foster family, but he couldn't go back. Said the drug guys would most likely hurt them to find out where he was. I was curious about the altercation and he said it went back to when he was eight years old when the gang shot and killed his brother and mother. Just awful. Said he witnessed it and they were after him to end the risk of being caught."

"Did he tell you what happened earlier that day?"

"Not exactly, but the sun was going down. He helped me gather some wood for a campfire and the subject just dropped. I told him that I was going to spear some flounder for dinner and take the rest home. He asked if he could help, and I told him I would pay him twenty-five dollars if we caught enough to take home. We did."

"What do you mean by spearing a fish?"

"Oh, this time of year the flounder come into the shallows to lay eggs at night. Maybe a foot or two deep. With a good light or a lantern you can wade through the water until you see the flounder's eyes looking up. Then, you just spear him with a sharp pole. We caught about ten or twelve."

"Sorry, go on with your story about Hector."

"We cleaned the fish and put all but three in the ice chest. I figured that I would eat one, and it would take two to make a meal for Hector. I asked him what he was going to do now. Said he didn't know, but he is very good at auto mechanics. Said he would like to know how to repair boat engines. Bingo! I knew that Uncle Bud was always looking for marine mechanics. We then cooked the flounder on the fire and slept in the dune buggy to get out of the crabs. As we were laying there staring at the stars, I offered for him to come with me but said he didn't want to get anyone else involved with his gang trouble. Said he would be down to talk to us in a few weeks. I went to sleep, got up early, and went home."

"And what time was that?

"I don't know, about eight or so I guess."

"That was around the time of the robbery and you had to drive right by the corner. Did you notice anything?"

"Yeah, now that you mentioned it. I saw some police lights flashing, but I needed to get some more ice for the flounders so I just went to the next store down the highway."

Detective Carlson looked over at Officer Thompson and said, "sounds like a solid alibi. Let's bust the big boy out of jail!"

As Hector moved into the conference room, everyone stood and shook his hand.

"We did find the punk that tried to kill you. The jerk is not dead, but I doubt he will ever regain the use of his right hand and the two punctured lungs will take a long time to heal. I am sure he didn't use his correct name so we cannot track his history. He did have a tattoo on his hand indicating a membership to the El Lobos. They did not know that the nurse could speak Spanish and while she was in the room she heard him threaten great harm to you. He said as soon as he gets well, he will be coming for you and kill anyone you have ever known. Hector, you must always be on the lookout."

Officer Thompson said, "Well Hector, what are you planning to do now?"

With a frown, he said, "I may need some help. When the bad guys start looking for me, my mom will be the first place they'll go. I can't protect her. Any suggestions?

"We will get the Corpus police to put her house on constant watch for a while. What this means is they will drive by every few hours. The gang will stay away if they see the cops are watching."

"Thanks. I wrote a letter to Mom a few minutes ago." He handed it to Officer Thompson. Could you deliver it to her tomorrow? I just told her that I was starting a new life on the West Coast and I would never come back and, of course, that I loved her like a real mom."

Bud stepped forward and announced, "Jack and I will be taking Hector back with us to the marina. From there, he can take as long as he needs to figure it out."

The detective added, "Good, I suggest you keep away from here and change your name. If he finds you, it will be a fight to the death."

Jack quickly jumped in, "We will be ready. Uncle Bud has a lot of guns and we all know how to use them."

They all said their goodbyes and well wishes and the three climbed into Bud's crew cab pickup and headed southwest.

Somewhere about halfway, Bud mentioned that he could keep a good mechanic busy and added, "Now listen up, this may sound generous, but I will expect something in return. Hector, you will need to finish your high school finals and then I will send you to tech school to learn diesel mechanics. Afterwards, you must work for me and you will do so until we are even. Deal?"

"Deal!"

A few more miles down the road, the subject was brought up by Bud stating, "I liked the idea of changing Hector's name. Let's not make it too easy on the El Lobos." Chuckling he added, "Not much we can do to change his size."

They all joined in the laughter, "Any suggestions?"

Jack said, "No doubt he is as big and strong as a bear. What do ya think?"

Hector said, "I like it and I will use my real mom's maiden name. She was an Italian named DeMarco. How does that sound, Bear DeMarco?

Jack jokingly asked, "Did she teach you how to cook Italian food?"

"Yes, but that was a long time ago. Maybe it'll come back to me."

Jack and Bud liked it and from there on the name "Hector Gomez" was never uttered again.

Chapter 10

Morning came with the sound of diesels warming up. Bud and Marge had been up for a couple of hours as this was a weekend and they knew that it would be a busy day. Bud was at the bait house. Marge and her cook, Maria, were getting ready for the breakfast rush.

Captain Isaiah Homes burst into the office and blurted out, "Morning Bud. Got a charter today and a crew member didn't show up. Is Jack available?"

"Go ask him, he is in the café."

Jack and Bear had just walked into the café looking like a couple of hungry puppies and sat down at a table. Captain Isaiah pulled up a chair, sat next to Jack, and mentioned the problem.

Jack shook his head and said, "Sorry, already got my plans but let me introduce you to Bear."

"Well, welcome to the Swordfish," said Captain Isaiah, "I need a deckhand for today. Pay you a hundred bucks and double that if we catch a marlin or sailfish."

Bear said, "I would like to go, but I don't know what to do."

"No problem, I have my lead guy. I'm just looking for some muscle."

Bear stood up and extended his massive hand, "Well, I am your man."

Captain Isaiah looked up at Bear and said, "Good Lord. Yeah, I think you will do very well. You need to be on my boat in fifteen minutes."

Marge walked over to the table and shouted to Maria, "Quick, get some breakfast over here. It looks like we've adopted another hungry lad."

Then she smiled at Bear and said, "Please, call me Aunt Marge."

Captain Isaiah Homes was one of the most successful charters operating out of Swordfish. The captain proudly gave Bear a tour of his boat. It was a fifty-five foot Hatteras with a fly-bridge, a tower, and a large rear fishing deck with two fighting chairs. It even had an air-conditioned cabin with a galley, a table with couches, and sleeping quarters. Twin diesel engines powered the vessel and had enough fuel capacity to stay out for a week. Bear was mesmerized. He had never seen such a boat. Yes, this was what he wanted.

He thought, *I can't believe that I could actually get paid to work on boats like this.*

The Captain introduced Bear to Juan, the lead deckhand.

He then explained, "The fishermen have paid a lot of money to fish today. Make them feel like kings. Make them want to come back. They paid two thousand dollars to fish. If they catch a marlin, sailfish, or tuna, they will pay an extra thousand dollars. If they hook one, it is our job to see that they get it in the boat. Juan will handle all the bait and rigging. If they hook a fish and get it next to the boat, it will be your job to gaff the fish." He reached down and picked up a long tube with a handle on one hand and a sharp hook on the other. "Just bend over the deck rail and use this hook. Stick him just behind the head. Be aggressive. You have to hook him the first try. Don't be shy. Then quickly lift it into the boat. A big one may weigh one hundred and fifty pounds. Did you get all of that?"

"Got it," said Bear.

Two middle-aged men soon arrived. One introduced himself as Jim Miller from Exxon and Flannigan O'Donnell from Ireland. They settled in the cabin, unpacked their gear, and started talking about drilling in the North Sea. Juan showed Bear how to handle the dock lines and in five minutes they were clearing the marina. Juan explained that they would not be fishing for maybe an hour.

"We need to get to the deep water where the fish live. Let me show you how to tie a hook into the bait fish so we can pull the bait through the water without ripping out the hook. It's called bait-rigging. We need to prepare maybe thirty of these hooks. Once we get one ready, we will put it into the ice chest to keep it fresh."

After a while, the color of the water changed from a dingy gray to a deep blue. The Captain yelled down to Juan to come up to the tower. Juan stuck his head inside the cabin and informed Jim and Flannigan to be ready.

The Captain began to change directions every few minutes and was watching for seagulls. Suddenly, Juan pointed and yelled at the Captain to notice a slick in the water. Juan quickly jumped down to the fishing deck where he found Jim and Flannigan already strapped into the fighting chairs. Juan grabbed a fishing rod and attached one of the baited fish hooks to the line. He cast it out and let off about one hundred yards of line and gave the pole to Flannigan. Juan did the same for Jim.

The Captain slowed the boat to about eight knots to find the right speed to let the baited hook to sink out of sight. Once satisfied, Juan grabbed one of the lines and clipped it to the starboard outrigger. It was like an extension pole to position the baited hook away from the wake of the boat and, upon getting a strike, the clip would release the line back to direct control of the reel. He did the same thing for the port outrigger line.

"Now we're fishing!" he said and climbed back up to the fly-bridge to watch for a strike.

On the third pass of the slick, the seagulls were still circling. Juan screamed, "STRIKE!" as he jumped back down to the fishing deck just as the outrigger released the line. "Set the hook!" he shouted to Flannigan. He then told Jim to quickly reel in his line to keep it out of the way.

Everyone was standing and watching as the fish plunged straight down and the Captain reduced speed. The big reel squealed as the line was feeding out against the reel's break and the pole began to bend. Flannigan was gripping it with all his might as the fish continued a heavy pull. Suddenly, the squeal stopped and the line went slack.

Juan yelled, "Reel it in. Get rid of the slack."

Just as Flannigan adjusted, the big fish jumped straight out of the water with his top fin fully extended and shook his head from side to side. It was a beautiful blue sailfish, maybe ten feet long. On his second jump, he jerked the hook lose and threw the bait fish back toward the boat. Gone.

Flannigan said, "Holy shit! That was exciting. Did I do something wrong?"

Captain Isaiah, put the boat in neutral and came down to the deck and said, "No, you did not do anything wrong. We don't get every fish back to the boat. He was a mighty fighter. Next time be ready to take up the slack quickly if he charges you. That is a challenging move."

They fished the rest of the day and did not get another strike. The Captain came down to the fishing deck and said, "They run in packs. It looks like our fish spooked his friends. They may be fifty miles from here by now."

He turned the boat to head back to the marina and he heard Flannigan say, "Well that was fun. It was worth every penny of it."

Back at the marina, most of the other charters were already in and docked.

Juan pointed out, "They were fishing for red snapper near and around the oil rigs."

Bear observed, "They must have been successful. Look at the cleaning station, it has a waiting line."

After securing the boat to the dock, Jim gave Captain Isaiah an envelope with two thousand dollars and they went to the café for a beer.

As Bear received his one hundred dollars, he thought, *Wow, that was the most fun job I ever had.*

That evening after the customers left, Marge was cooking some of the flounder that Jack had brought back from Corpus Christi. She stuffed each flounder with a mix of crab meat, shrimp, and bread crumbs and broiled each in the oven to perfection. She, Bear, Jack, and Uncle Bud sat down at a table, each with a bottle of cold beer. They ate every last morsel of the flounder. After Maria cleared the table, Bud led the discussion on Bear's options. He announced that he had located a marine tech school in New Orleans.

He explained, "I know a marina operator there and he told me about an eighteen-month course covering engines, transmissions, hydraulics, and drives. You would be very marketable after getting an Associate's degree. Cost you about ten thousand bucks including room and board. Remember, the deal is that you must come back here and pay me back before you venture off with someone else."

"I can't believe you would do that for me. Why?" asked Bear.

"Why not? I will get my money back plus some. Call it an investment."

"I think I'll work for Captain Isaiah until I leave for school. I need some spending money."

They all clinked their beer mugs and saluted Bear.

Jack said, "Here's to you, big guy."

Chapter 11

Christmas at the Swordfish was a little different than most people experienced throughout the world. The charter business was mostly shut down. All but the "Live Aboards" were gone, and their boats were shut in for the season. Winter in South Padre was the most pleasant time of the year. The gentle south breeze kept the temperatures in the seventies with very little humidity. Marge had Bud and Jack put up strings of Christmas lights along each dock walkway and had a big tree decorated in the dining hall. Bear had just finished his first six months at the tech school and was on Christmas break. He was not due back until the middle of January. It was good times for the Mahan family. Jack even got a Christmas card from his father.

Christmas dinner was a time to review last year and talk about the future. Bud announced that he had some big plans for the Swordfish. He would be installing a new dock row to accommodate up to ten more boats and he already had lease deposits for eight of them.

He looked at Bear with a big smile and said, "I am also installing a boat lift and repair facility. We will be able to service up to seventy footers. I think it has your name on it."

Bear let out a big hoot and said, "It's nice to have a job lined up already."

Marge looked over at Jack and asked, "What are your plans?"

He looked at everyone and answered, "I sort of like the job I have. What's wrong with beachcombing for another year or two?"

Marge came back with, "Why don't you find a nice girl and settle down?"

He laughed and said, "They demand too much time. Ya' know me, I like my freedom. Blimey, the dune buggy, the beach house and Marge's cooking, it can't get much better."

Part Four –

The Coast Guard Connection

Chapter 12

The view from the thirty-eighth floor of downtown Dallas was spectacular. The floor-to-ceiling windows offered a panoramic view of the financial district and the city hub. Sitting in the firm's private conference room were the three founding partners of the law practice, Sampson, Boone, and Holt. With spit-shined boots propped upon the highly polished, rosewood meeting table, they were privately celebrating ending the year with over eight and a half million dollars in undistributed profits. Life was good.

In just ten years the firm grew from the three partners to a powerhouse money-maker with offices in Dallas, Houston, and New Orleans. They were supporting over two hundred attorneys, staff, and legal assistants. The firm specialized in mergers and acquisitions, intellectual properties like patents and copyrights, real estate, and maritime Law. The partners believed their success was the ability to attract and recruit the top talent available from the most reputable universities throughout the United States. To keep growing, they were continuously hiring recruits to replenish the normal attrition of lower staff attorneys and, of course, hiring for new business opportunities.

Bazaar was the description of the firm's recruiting practices. They combed the best grad schools for promising young attorneys to invite for interviews. Once they were ready to make an offer, they required one last consultation with upper management. Famously, they did not discriminate male versus female, but they would separate them for the last interview. The female senior managers would handle the final meeting and had the last word. The males, on the other hand, were managed by the founders. They strived to find candidates that would fit in with the highly aggressive atmosphere of the firm. If they projected the survival of the fittest attitude. An associate once heard a partner stating, "We don't want any panty-waist sissy doing work for our corporate clients. We want an image of dominance." The system had worked for a long time.

Handling the final interviews for the female recruits were two senior partners, Taylor Carmichael and Eva Sanchez. Taylor was the firm's most senior partner and Eva just had a mean streak. If any of their clients went to trial, she was the firm's go-to attorney. Eva was a ruthless litigator. Most of her cases were settled out of court as she had a record of never losing a single case. They looked for the same "take-no-prisoners" attitude in any candidate they interviewed.

Rex Sampson and his two founding partners met in college and stayed close friends, both professionally and socially. They were all active sportsmen and realized if they pooled their money, they could afford some extreme luxurious hobbies. Shared items included a hunting lodge in Montana, a home in Maui, and a condo in Vail. They all loved sport-fishing. Visiting each of their private offices was like going into a man cave. One would agree that a lot of testosterone was on display in the form of animals killed and fish caught.

It was at the conference room table that Rex and his two partners agreed to purchase a new yacht. It was to be large and luxurious enough to entertain clients on fishing trips, but functional enough to be used for family cruises anywhere in the Caribbean or South America. It should not require a full-time crew but on most trips they would hire a captain, chef, and a deckhand. They settled on a sixty-five foot Viking Luxury Sportfish, priced at a little over two million dollars. It had a teak cockpit with state-of-the-art electronics and luxurious mezzanine seating. It also had a spacious salon, three staterooms, and a separate crew area. It was astonishingly beautiful and could cruise for hours at thirty knots. They visited the factory in New Jersey and immediately made the deal. The company arranged to make the delivery at the Galveston City Marina.

The call to the Swordfish Marina was just in time to secure the last big slip on the new dock. The bank wired the funds and Rex couldn't wait. He informed Bud Mahan that he planned to be at Swordfish sometime between Christmas and New Year's Day.

Boone and Holt had already committed to a family ski trip at the condo in Vail, so Rex volunteered to deliver the yacht to the Swordfish. He was a qualified sailor with loads of experience operating large boats. He would take possession of the craft in Galveston just after Christmas. There he would be trained and given a day-long sea trial or shakedown cruise before final transfer of ownership. He wanted to take enough time to learn most of the systems on the yacht adequately.

He was up to the challenge and anxious to get it down to Swordfish as quickly as possible. It would be a two-day trip. The first day would be to Corpus Christi and he would spend the night docked at the T-Heads near the downtown hotels. He estimated that this would be about a seven- to eight-hour trip, depending on the weather. Completing the journey to Port Isabel and the Swordfish Marina the next day would be somewhat shorter.

To complete the yacht for their use, he hired an artist to paint its name on the transom, "*Judgement*".

Chapter 13

The partners were in the final interview process with a very promising recruit from the Vanderbilt School of Law. He had just graduated at the top of his class with a Masters from Harvard. The three partners discussed the testosterone issue and decided that it would be perfect to take this young man on the trip from Galveston to the Swordfish marina. After two days, they would be one hundred percent sure if he would fit their requirements. After all, to be safe, Rex needed someone else to go along. The young man's name was Charles Theodore Buckley III and he went by Teddy

On December 27th, Teddy flew to Galveston, took a taxi to the public marina, and found Rex on the new boat.

Like a proud father, he yelled out to Teddy, "Welcome to *Judgement*. Please come aboard."

"Thanks," said Teddy, "I don't know much about boating."

"That's okay, let me show you around, but we need to depart as quickly as possible."

"Do I need to wear a life jacket?"

"If you want to, but this is a big yacht and wearing a life vest is not a requirement. But I need to give you a safety tour. It is required." With much patience, Rex pointed out fire extinguishers, floatation gear, the marine radio, the first aid kit, and, of course, the lifeboat. "It is designed for even the most novice sailor to use. See this plastic cover. Just pull the cover out of the way and push the red button. The lifeboat will be inflated and lowered to the water. It has an outboard motor, so all you do is get in the boat and turn the switch to start, just like a car. Now, do you feel better?"

"Yes, I am ready. Let's go."

In less than twenty minutes, Rex, Teddy, and *Judgement* were out of the harbor and heading out to the Gulf of Mexico.

Teddy climbed the stairs up to the cockpit and found a seat next to Rex and said, "This is nice. You have an excellent view from up here."

The first hint of seasickness came when Teddy went down to use the bathroom. The room began to blur and move. He did not come back up, but instead he sat down at the galley table. It didn't help. As Teddy could feel his stomach beginning to churn, he looked for a bucket. He chose the galley sink. Teddy made it, but it was a mess and smelled awful. Looking at it, he threw up again.

Wiping his mouth and climbing back up to the cockpit, he looked at Rex and said, "I guess I had a small attack of seasickness. I think I will stay up here."

Rex answered, "That won't work. We move around a lot up here. It's best to go down to the fishing deck and strap yourself into one of the fighting chairs. If you get sick again, just lean over the back of the boat and vomit all you want."

About halfway, Rex put the boat on autopilot and came down to check on the young man. Teddy looked green but was hanging in there. Rex stepped into the cabin and was disgusted at the smell. He cleaned it up as best he could, got a cold bottle of water, and gave it to Teddy on the way back up to the cockpit.

Okay, he thought, *give him a chance. A lot of people get seasick.*

Coming through the jetties and into Corpus Christi bay, the movement of the boat calmed and Teddy began to move around. After Rex moored the boat in one of the visitor slips, Teddy quickly exited and sat on the dock.

Rex helped him up and said, "Come on. I'll get you checked in to the hotel and you can clean up. You need to have a meal soon to replenish your strength. I'll also get you some seasick pills. Tomorrow will be better."

Rex and Teddy were up early and met at the breakfast bar.

"Well Teddy, you are looking better today."

"Thanks, Mr. Sampson. Yeah, yesterday was rather embarrassing."

"No problem son, I got seasick in the beginning too. Here, take these pills. Most of the time they will fix the problem. Let's get going. We have a long day ahead."

As they pulled out of the intercoastal channel and through the jetties, Rex noticed that the seas were getting angry. A check with the weather station confirmed a front was building. He thought, *Teddy is not going to like this trip either.*

The boat was handling the rough seas very well, but the wind was getting worse. Even so, Teddy was hanging on to the fighting chair and making the best of it. Rex decided to duck into the intercoastal for the remainder of the trip. It was a little longer, but it should be smoother.

Teddy noticed a change in the wind and thought that they were approaching the marina, so he climbed up into the cockpit.

Rex said, "We are not there yet. It's going to get worse before we get into the intercoastal canal waters."

"I'm okay," said Teddy, but immediately began getting sick again. When it hit, it was violent. Vomit exploded out of his mouth like a gusher from Yosemite and hit the windshield and instrument panel and then bounced into the hands and chest of Rex. Teddy fell to his knees, with vomit dripping from his mouth and cried, "Mr. Sampson, I am so sorry about this."

He looked up to see Rex grabbing his chest and heard him say, "Oh my God, I think I'm having a heart attack!"

Rex slipped down to the level of Teddy and said, "You are in control now. Just get us through the jetties and into the intercoastal waters then shut us down and call the Coast Guard."

Teddy grabbed the wheel and pulled himself to his feet. He thought, *I have never driven a boat ever. What are these handles?*

The wind was blowing the boat directly into large granite rocks. The more Teddy turned the wheel, the more he positioned the boat for a broadside collision with the jetties. He tried one of the handles and found that it would speed up or slow down the engine.

Why do I have two handles?

By using only one engine, he had accidentally positioned the rear of the boat not ten feet from the first rock. Seconds later, a loud crack and vibration hit the entire vessel. Both engines stopped and it settled between two boulders and the main jetty. The wind continued to push the boat into the danger and the loud crunching and cracking noises continued.

I have got to get help.

Forgetting about seasickness, he looked across the channel and saw what looked like a car or jeep on the beach.

Maybe they can help.

He remembered the lifeboat and he located the switch. In an instant, the inflatable boat was in the water and Teddy was climbing down into the driver's seat. He reached over to the control panel and turned the starter switch. Thankfully, the engine came to life just before it too was pushed into the rocks. Teddy gunned it and steered directly to the beach.

Jack, Bear, and Blimey were on a leisurely Christmas beach drive in the dune buggy.

Bear said, "Look out there, Jack. That boat's in trouble and it seems like a lifeboat is coming this way." A check with the binoculars confirmed the situation.

Teddy ran the inflatable up onto the beach.

Jack yelled, "Kill the engine."

Teddy jumped out and ran to the dune buggy as he began shouting and pointing, "Help me. The captain had a heart attack and the boat is in danger on the jetties."

Jack immediately reached for his medical kit and Bear ran to the inflatable to turn it around. Jack yelled at Teddy, "Are you coming?"

Teddy said, "No, I cannot go back to that boat."

"It's up to you," responded Jack. "Blimey, stay here and protect the dune buggy. Let's go Bear."

Chapter 14

Jack and Bear were on the troubled boat in ten minutes. They found the Captain in the cockpit and noticed that the ship was beginning to take on water from the rear. Jack found an aspirin bottle in his medical case and gave it to Bear.

"Give him a single pill, I am going to look for a way out of here."

He moved to the bow and found the primary anchor and a hydraulic powered windlass anchor winch. Jack realized they could not manually handle the standard chain and anchor as it was much too heavy. But he did find a lightweight day anchor and about two hundred yards of braided three-fourths-inch nylon line. He tied the end of the line near the windlass and called for Bear.

"I am going to pull the lifeboat around to the bow. Hand me the anchor and the coil of line. As I take it out, see if you can get an engine started. The props are on the rocks so be sure to keep it in neutral. We need to power up the hydraulic system. When I drop the anchor, loop the line over the winch and start taking up the slack. If we are lucky, we can pull the boat off the jetties."

Jack pointed the lifeboat directly into the wind and began letting out the line as he made headway. At the end of the line, he dropped the anchor and returned to the boat.

Bear was able to start the port engine even though it was halfway underwater. He monitored the engine controls in the cockpit as Jack worked on the anchor system. He stepped on the windlass anchor switch and it came alive. Jack smiled as the winch began to take in the anchor line. Quickly the anchor stuck in the mud and its rope became as tight as a guitar string. Jack knew if it broke, he would suffer from the force of the line recoiling and knocking him into the water and onto the jetties. To be cautious, he would take up a few feet and stop then take up a few more feet. Finally, he felt the boat jerk and roll slightly.

On the next try, the boat came free and moved sideways somewhat. At this point, Jack saw the line had lost some tension as the ship freed itself from the rocks. He reeled in about thirty more feet and stopped to watch. The anchor was holding and the boat was safe for a while. The crack in the rear was continuing to let in some water but the sump pump was discharging as much water as the boat was taking in. It would be okay as long as the batteries stay charged.

Rex was moving around somewhat but still laying down. Bear continued to talk to him while Jack called the Coast Guard.

Chapter 15

Commander Brad McCormick was flying a MEDEVAC-capable. HH-65 Dolphin helicopter and had just finished a training exercise at the Naval Air Station near Corpus Christi. He still had his full crew and medical supplies when the call came in from Headquarters.

He answered the radio, "Roger base, we will take this. Tell them that our ETA is twenty-two minutes and give me the position of the nearest Coast Guard cutter that offers emergency room capability."

"You are in luck Commander; the USGCC Eagle is only five miles from the target."

"Roger. Tell them that I will be bringing in a middle age man with an apparent heart attack."

"Good luck Sir."

Hovering over the yacht and looking down from the air, Commander McCormick was pleased as he communicated to his crew, "The craft is now out of jetty trouble and it is large enough to get the cage on the front deck."

Two rescue crewmen were standing in the basket as the helicopter lowered it. It only took a few minutes to secure Rex in the basket and lift him into the aircraft. The crew explained to Jack and Bear that the helicopter would be back shortly to address the needs of the boat. They began asking questions.

"This is a beautiful boat. Is it yours?"

Jack took the lead in answering the questions, "No sir, I think the boat belongs to the man with the heart attack. We were on the beach over there when the lifeboat came to us."

"Who was driving the lifeboat?"

"Don't know sir. It was a terrified young man. I think he ran off after we got into the lifeboat."

"Ran off?"

"Yes sir. He said something like he never wanted to see that boat again."

"Do you know where the boat was going?"

"Not exactly, but we were expecting a new sport-fishing boat to be delivered to the Swordfish marina sometime this week. This magnificent yacht must be it."

"I need to look around a bit while we are waiting for our lift. You guys can just stay here in the cockpit."

"Sure, it's not my boat. Do what you need to do, but we need a ride back to our dune buggy.

Commander McCormick radioed back to his crew. "Looks like the Captain did have a heart attack, but he is stabilized now and should be back on his feet in a week or two. The two boys saved his life and saved his boat from a total loss. We all will owe the guys a big Coast Guard 'thank you'. I am bringing back some experts to get the boat ready to tow. Be back in about twenty minutes."

"Roger, we found nothing here but a new boat. Everything looks legit. Out"

Soon the crew members were exchanged, Jack and Bear were loaded in, and the helicopter ferried them back to the dune buggy.

As they were stepping down to the beach, the Commander said, "I like what you guys did. I want to bring you into our office and let you meet the rest of the Coast Guard team."

"Yes, that would be interesting. We'd love to do that."

Part Five –

Salvage Junker Gets a Facelift

Chapter 16

Six months had passed since Rex Sampson's heart attack and the resulting collision of the firm's luxury yacht, *Judgement*. Rex was now working but had reduced his load down to only eight hours per day. The firm's sixty-five-foot Viking Luxury Sportfish had completed its factory repairs and was in new condition, safely secured in her new home at the Swordfish Marina. But for Rex, it was more than just the boat and his health. It was the damage to his pride. It was still raw. He had a lot of time to do some serious thinking about his life and his firm. He made a list.

First was Teddy. Rex thought, *Yes, he did not fit the rough and tumbled profile that they were looking for. But he did have the courage and smarts to launch the lifeboat and find help. It is likely if Teddy had become paralyzed with fear, the boat would be totaled and both Teddy and I would have died.*

Rex contacted Teddy to thank him and to extend the job offer. Teddy voiced appreciation for the call but informed him that he had already accepted another offer. He tactfully told Rex that his firm was not a good fit for him. Rex offered a good luck remark but did not add any additional comments. As he put the receiver down in the cradle, he thought, *Good, I feel better already*!

Next on the list was to face his two partners and admit that he was not Superman. He should not have taken the boat out without a professional captain to at least supervise the trip. He certainly needed someone with more experience than Teddy. With that said, he suffered through a few good-natured verbal jabs. After administering adequate punishment, they quickly checked the calendar to plan for their first fishing trip.

Rex also wanted to thank Commander Brad McCormick and the young men from Swordfish personally. They were actually the ones who saved the day for him.

The first call was to the Coast Guard and found that, by promotion, the Commander was now Captain of the new Marine Safety Security Team (MSST), located on the Houston ship channel. After a respectful conversation, the Captain asked Rex for a favor, "Would you contact Bud Mahan at the Swordfish and invite him and the boys to attend a special meeting here in Houston?"

"Sure, what can I tell them?

The Captain outlined a few details and finished the conversation with, "It's a new program we are putting together. I think it would be a perfect fit for the guys."

Bud Mahan answered the phone and the two exchanged pleasant greetings. Rex asked about the young men. Bud confirmed that Jack was still doing his beachcombing thing and Bear had graduated from the Tech School with an Associates Certificate. He was finding work at the marina and was keeping busy.

Rex asked, "Before the sport-fishing season gets hectic, I would like you, Jack, and Bear to join us at the Coast Guard facility in Houston. Commander, now Captain Brad McCormick is running the MSST effort. I just talked to him and he would like to organize a meeting to discuss a special project they are putting together. He will send a Coast Guard aircraft down to deliver you to Houston and also arrange for someone to pick you up there to drive you to the facility."

Bud asked, "What is MSST?"

"He said it's a new effort to detect and intercept criminal or illegal events well before they threaten our shores. It is called the Marine Safety and Security Team. I don't know much more, but McCormick said he had been thinking about the boys. He was quite impressed with them. Said it could be a very profitable opportunity for them. He wants you to come and listen. If you are not interested, no problem."

Bud said, "That would be worth the time. When does he want us?"

"I will call you back shortly. By the way, I will also attend the meeting."

"Okay, I'll tell the boys."

A few days later, a small Learjet with Coast Guard colors taxied and parked next to the private terminal at Brownsville Airport. Neither Jack nor Bear had ever been on an airplane and were rightfully excited. Lieutenant Mills gave them a quick tour and informed them the trip to Ellington Air Base would only take ninety minutes.

Bud looked confused, and ask, "Why Ellington?"

"Oh, it is the nearest military airfield. It's neighboring NASA and not far from the Coast Guard facility. You will be meeting with Captain McCormick there."

After being ushered into a large conference room, it was almost eleven o'clock. Already seated were several high-ranking Coast Guard officers plus Rex and Captain McCormick. After the introductions, two assistants brought in several trays of sandwiches and soft drinks.

"Might as well make this a working lunch," said the Captain.

After finishing the meal, McCormick stood up and began the meeting,

"Thank you for coming. To start with, this is a classified meeting and the subject matter is highly sensitive. Please do not discuss the details with anyone who is not involved with this project. Be advised, the President of the United States and the Secretary of State have approved and activated a program called The Marine Safety and Security Team and referred to as MSST. It will employ dedicated teams to prohibit and neutralize potential threats, with force if needed."

He continued, "To be specific, our task will be to detect and intercept criminal or unlawful events well before they threaten our shores. We want to capture or kill the bad guys before they step on land and cause havoc to our citizens."

Everyone was intently listening.

He paused and said, "Frankly, the illegal drug industry is kicking our butt. They know our laws and have hired the best attorneys to fight against enforcement. Right now, we cannot stop any commercial or private vessel in international waters. Which means they can sail their supply ships anywhere freely if they stay outside the twelve-mile boundary. They will have a local ship, say a fishing boat, sneak out to the supply ship to exchange cash for ordered narcotics. The fishing boat will then bring back the order to the local master dealer. If the local boat is busted, the supply boat does not get hurt. It's a small hit to them. They have the cash and they still have the mass inventory of drugs to move on to the next location."

Rex interrupted with a question, "I can understand the problem, but how do we fit in with this situation?"

"Excellent timing with that question. We are thinking about starting a new program. You know the Coast Guard is limited in what we can do and where we can go. We have to live with the rules or the arrest will be thrown out in court. It is almost impossible to do anything proactive. Typically we are called in when something has already gone wrong. Yes, we sometimes catch drug dealing, human smuggling, or even commercial poaching. But even at that we are not being proactive, just generally responding to a tip."

He took a moment to look around the table and said, "We can, however, work with contractors just like the military. The Marines and the Navy have been using contractors for years in areas of security, surveillance, or clean-up. We have some government funds to experiment with, but it would not be enough actually to set anything in place. These young men are perfect for what we have in mind to start a covert contractor company. You will be the first contractors, sort of a prototype."

"Really, what do you envision?" asked Bud.

"Well, let's assume a contractor has the tools and training. If they were to start a salvage company and do enough salvage work to be legit, they could go almost anywhere without restrictions and never be identified as a government or police activity. They could be our eyes and ears for incoming shipments. Hell, they could even set up a sting operation to attract the bad guys."

Everyone in the room was dead silent until Uncle Bud said with a heavy tone, "That sounds like it might be dangerous."

"Anything to do with the ocean is dangerous. Being a cop is dangerous. Consider they are of the exact age to join the military. Now *that* is dangerous! Besides, they will be armed and the Coast Guard will be closely monitoring their activity."

"Okay, but what's in it for them?"

"They will be highly paid independent contractors. But the best part is if they assist in catching a gangster, I mean a real high-level cartel boss, there will be a huge reward. If they help catch a shipment of narcotics, the government will pay them twenty percent of the street value. Say they bust a shipment, with our help, worth two million dollars, they would get four hundred thousand!"

Uncle Bud whistled, "Boom! Now I see where you are going with this."

Rex spoke up, "I have a couple of questions. Number one, how much money would be needed to set this up? Number two, what kind of training and support will the Coast Guard offer?"

"On the first question, the majority of the money will be spent on the boat and accessories. I see getting an old junker and redoing it to meet the minimum needs of a salvage boat. But the significant expenses will be spent on electronics, weapons, and camouflage. My guess is a total of three hundred thousand dollars. As far as the training, I will get a special exemption for them to go through basic training with the next available class. Then each will specialize in specific skills, such as marine mechanics, electronics, or to qualify for a Coast Guard approved captain's license. Knowing these boys, Bear would become an expert in diesel engines and transmissions, Jack should get a captain's license, and both would become highly trained in marine electronics and navigation. Of course, the Coast Guard will pay for the training and weapons."

Rex cleared his throat and said, "Well, saving my life and the two million dollar fishing boat is well worth that investment. But now that I know the purpose here, I must say that I have a special hatred for the drug cartels. Three years ago, I lost both my son and daughter on the same night by a drug overdose. I would do anything to be a part of destroying those monsters. For that reason, I will bump up the contribution to half a million."

The room was stunned.

Rex finished, "Oh, by the way, my law firm will do all the legal work and represent them if they get in trouble, also on a no-charge basis."

Uncle Bud looked around the table again and said, "Before we start spending money and chasing bad guys, I think we need to hear from the boys."

Now all eyes were on Jack and Bear.

Jack leaned back in the big conference chair and said, "Now let me get this straight and review what I have just heard. It looks like I am going to have to quit my beachcombing job and Bear is not going to work for Uncle Bud. But on the other hand, if we do this we are going to get to play like we are James Bond with high tech boats and weapons, chasing the drug cartel all over the high seas. Rex here is putting up the money and the President of the United States has approved the Coast Guard to train and help us if we get in trouble. We will be using a camouflaged battleship and if we catch a thug with a truckload of dope, we get a ka-zillion bucks. All of this with no greater risk of being killed than becoming a marine? I don't know. Bear are you in?"

"Hell yea, I would love nothing more than getting my hands on the dope man."

Uncle Bud jumped in, "I think you just drew four threes in a Seven Card Stud poker game. Go for it."

"Jack stood up and said, "We're in. Where do we sign up?"

Rex added, "My firm will represent you, of course at no charge. We will get started this week and have a contract ready for signatures next week."

Captain McCormick stood up and reached out to shake hands with the boys and Bud, "We will start a search for a suitable old clunker to use as the salvage boat. We should have a few choices to look at next week while we are signing the contract. Get your personal business finished as soon as possible. A new recruiting class will be starting basic training in three weeks. You must be at the USCG Training Center in Camp May, New Jersey by then."

Chapter 17

Their next ride on the Learjet wasn't quite as thrilling as the first. Considering the decision would change the rest of their lives, they had a lot to think about during the short flight. Rex Sampson had called, confirming the contract was complete and that he would attend the meeting.

Captain McCormick and Coast Guard JAG officer Lieutenant Keller were waiting when they entered the conference room. Rex arrived a few minutes later.

As the meeting began, the JAG officer stood to address the gathering, "Gentlemen, I have been working with Mr. Sampson's firm for the last several days and we have worked out a contract which we both find acceptable. It is similar to other contract service agreements used by the Marines and Navy. The Captain and I will step out of the conference room to give Mr. Sampson the opportunity to explain the details. Let us know when you finish."

After the door closed, Rex said, "I won't confuse you with the legal jargon but let me just outline the basic relationship."

"Sounds good to me," Bud said. "We trust you to protect us as best as you can."

"In simple terms, this contract lays out the legal relationship between the U.S. Government and you and the boys. You will form a corporation. The contract will be between the Coast Guard and the corporation. You will have the authority to work independently without the need of close supervision of the MSST. They will share data with you and vice versa. You may discover your own leads or MSST can pass along a lead or outline a mission. Other than that, you are an independent contractor. You may not make an arrest but you can hold a suspect captive until the Coast Guard arrives. You may not use lethal force unless you are threatened or feel the situation will escalate to a dangerous level. The government needs as much distance as possible to detach the Coast Guard from your work."

Jack responded, "That makes sense."

"Your payments will be of many types such as monthly fees as outlined in the contract, expense reimbursements, special assignments, rewards, and special bonus incentives. Insurance is up to you, which I will arrange with our agents to get you the finest medical and accidental insurance as possible."

"How much control will they have with our missions?"

"They will identify and help plan each mission and can terminate a mission at any time and they can call you in for help as needed."

"Can we get fired?"

"Yes, it is a contractual relationship. The government can terminate the contract if they determine the test program is not working as they had hoped. They can also terminate the contract if you do not perform your assignments. It is a government program. Therefore it may not get funded at some future date. But for the next year or so, you will be given a lot a latitude on how you run the corporation."

"Anything we need to do right now?"

"Yes," Rex said smiling, "you need to name the corporation so we can do the legal work to make it official and then to complete and sign the contract.

Bear said, "We have been talking about a name all last week, and we settled on one. What do you think about *Sanford Salvage and Water Repairs*?

"You mean like the old T.V. show about a junkyard?

"Yeah, but it is not a junkyard. It is a junk boat plus we do in-the-water repairs."

"I like it. I'll put it in the contract."

After a few more loose ends were tied up and explained, Rex called Captain McCormack and the JAG officer back in.

"Are you satisfied with the contract?"

"Yes," said Jack.

The Captain responded, "Mr. Sampson and Lieutenant Keller, I think the contract is complete. You are welcome to stay, but if you need to attend to other matters you may go."

Both said goodbye and good luck and exited the conference room.

The Captain said, "We have some more issues to discuss today such as selecting a boat and getting you ready for basic training."

"Good, what boat did you find?"

"We got lucky, said the Captain. "Let me show you some pictures."

Everyone passed the pictures while standing around the table.

"This was an early picture of a fifty-five-foot utility boat used for various purposes around the European coastline. Its last use was as a tugboat to pull international shipping barges. Its last assignment was to hall machinery parts and tools to the U.S. As it pulled into a New Jersey harbor, one engine exploded and caught fire. Both the boat and barge required towing into the docks. Later the boat was judged a total loss. It was at a salvage sale when we bought it for the scrap value of the steel and it now sits in our shipyard located in Curtis Bay, Maryland."

"Will you be able to repair the engines?"

"Oh no, not at all. You have the budget to do a major makeover and we have the facilities and available surplus inventory to do the repairs at minimal cost. We don't build luxury yachts but we can build fast military ships. The first thing we will do is gut the entire engine room. We will clean the insides down to the steel and finish it with white epoxy. It will look like an operating room when we are through cleaning."

Jack asked, "Just the engine room?"

"No, the entire below deck area. The engine room only takes up about a quarter of the space below deck. When we finish, you will have a large area below deck to store most anything you may need such as an inflatable high-speed attack boat, a complete scuba support station with compressors and associated gear, of course a workshop and tool room with welding capabilities, and maybe even motorcycles,. We are not going to furnish this out, but it will be there for whatever you want."

Bear piped up and ask, "What engines will you be installing?"

"You guys are going to love this. We believe that you might get into situations that would call for a very agile and fast boat, either for catching bad guys or getting away from them. We checked our surplus inventory and found some engines and drivetrains. So we are going to install two turbocharged Cummings diesel engines with an output of over seven hundred HP each. Combine that with military transmissions and props and you should get a top speed of maybe forty-five knots or about twice the speed of standard commercial yachts of the same size."

"You mentioned navigation and electronics at our last meeting. What will we have here?"

"That will come later in the build process. But we will retrofit the entire bridge to match up with your new needs. Just remember, we need to know exactly where you are at all times. Plus we must have the ability to talk to you on secure radio communications privately."

"This all sounds great. What about the weapons?"

"You will be fully armed. Unless you are up against a military ship, you should have the advantage. But, like the electronics, we will address this later.

Do you guys approve of the boat and the plans and may we move ahead?"

All agreed and shook the Captain's hand.

"Now," he said, "let's talk about basic training. You will be normal Coast Guard recruits. We are not going to give you an advantage. If you cannot make it through basic, the deal is off. Do you understand?"

The boys confirmed with a nod of the head.

"If anyone finds out that you are not in the Coast Guard, the deal is off. Do you also understand this?"

Again they agreed.

"The first two weeks will be physical fitness and attitude training. After that, you will be doing group training in shooting, self-defense, and boating safety. Next, you will begin your selected skills training. The whole process will take six months. At that time your boat will be finished and you will disappear from your recruiting class. The next time I should hear from you should be when you deliver the ship to its home port, the Swordfish Marina.

"During the six months, you will have leave, or time off, to do what you please. I would suggest you spend that time in Curtis Bay, Maryland at the boatyard. By then, you will be needed to make some decisions before finishing the boat."

"Sounds like we have a hectic schedule."

"Yes, but to change the subject, I must warn you of how dangerous the project could get. Please listen carefully to what I am about to say. Lawless scumbags run the drug industry. They have no problem with killing and sometimes they do it for fun. They are also very vindictive. If you kill one of them, they will try to kill four of you. If they know who you are, where you live, or where you work, they will track you down and extract maximum punishment."

Bear spoke up, "I know for a fact that you are correct. I saw them kill my mother and brother and they are still trying to find me because I might someday testify against them."

The Captain said, "Yes, I know your history. The point is you must remain unknown to them and the public must not know that you are government contractors."

"What do you mean?" asked Bud.

"To the public, you must be a small salvage company. You may live a normal life, but I would suggest you always be careful and pay attention to strangers. When you need to come in contact with the bad guys, always take steps to go undercover. We will devise a way to camouflage your boat. Think of a chameleon lizard. It can change colors to make them less visible. To the public, your ship is an old salvage boat. But when confronting an enemy your ship will change to look like a lethal military badass without any markings to associate it as part of the U.S. Military or the Coast Guard."

"How are you going to do that?"

"We have some ideas, but they are not entirely worked out. For example, the salvage boat will have old tires hanging over the sides to protect other ships from damage while you are doing repairs. You know, junky-looking. Under the tires and out of site will be a military look, think of jungle camouflage. When you punch a button, the hydraulic system will bring the tires up and over the sides of the boat and store them out of sight. It would also change the look of the tower and bridge and bring out the fixed machine guns on the bow and stern.

"You can do that?"

"A few years ago we toyed with the theory."

"Sort of like Clark Kent stepping into a phone booth and coming out being Superman?"

"Yes, I like the analogy, but the boat is not the only thing that must change. You also need a disguise. You cannot let them see you as a normal person."

"What can we do?"

"This is much easier than the boat. You will change into military combat clothing with vests, helmets, and either grease camo on your face or a military face mask. If you want, you could even design your own disguise. But the point is that the bad guys cannot make a connection with your real-world looks. You will have a class in the art of camouflage during basic training. You will learn about false teeth, hair, and beards. That is the fun part. You need to become masters of disguise."

"This seems bigger and more difficult than we thought."

"Maybe, but the rewards are huge. I think you guys are up to it but you must be committed. You have until Basic Training begins to back out. If you are in, I will drop in to see you occasionally during the training. Good luck. I think your driver is ready to take you back to the Learjet."

They all once again shook hands as they were leaving the conference room.

Chapter 18

Wearing their best beachwear, Jack and Bear made their way to the indoctrination center with hours to spare. They were given the standard issue Basic Training fatigues, shoes, underwear, and a universal white Navy hat. On the next table, they were given a giant duffel bag and told to write their names across the middle of it with the black marker dangling on the end of a string.

"Now, go to the dressing area, stuff your street clothes in the duffel, and put on your basic training uniform. When you finished, go to the next room and meet your new hairdresser. After that, come back here and take a seat with the other folks."

Bear pointed to Jack and laughed, "Looking sharp with your new hat and hairdo."

Jack waved at Bear with only his middle finger, laughed back, and said, "You too."

Just at that time, a very rude brute of a man came in and said, "Hello girls, my name is Chief Weatherford but you will always address me as Sir. Welcome to Hell Week. Let me escort you to your living quarters for the next few weeks. I am sure you will enjoy sharing your life with thirty-one other sissy recruits. Evening mess is at eighteen-hundred hours. You will need to figure out what time that is. Just to let you know, this is the last time I will be nice to you."

Bear looked over at Jack and whispered, "I think I'm going to like this guy."

Jack just rolled his eyes and said nothing.

The next few days were exactly as advertised, Hell Week. The class size was thirty-two and they were from all over the U.S. but the majority of them were from the East Coast. It was twenty-six males and six intimidating-looking females. The girls had separate barracks but that was the only break they received.

Physical conditioning was the only thing on Chief Weatherford's mind for the first week. It was jogging, calisthenics, the obstacle course, lunch, and doing it all again with a five-mile run before lights out in the barracks. No one dropped out but Bear was always near the last on the running parts and was given holy hell by the Chief. The following week eased a little and they added shooting, self-defense, and boating safety skills. Jack was the best shot in the class and Bear was the champ of defensive training.

The end of two weeks of boot camp, as the recruits called it, concluded with sort of a graduation ceremony and the class was given a day off before they broke up into the specific skills training. They were moved out of the recruit barracks and into quarters located near the individual skill centers. Jack and Bear shared the first session on shipboard electronics including radar, navigation, vessel-to-vessel radio, and secure operational communications.

As planned, Jack and Bear separated for the second session. Bear attended technical skill training for engines and drivetrains while Jack was fulfilling the requirements to earn Coast Guard Captains Credentials. The license would certify Jack in authorization to command a vessel up to twenty-five gross tons as a master, captain, or skipper and an included an endorsement for commercial towing and assistance.

In the evenings, Jack and Bear took advantage of the Coast Guard facilities and received scuba certification. They thought that being able to dive could come in handy.

Jack and Bear spent the free time visiting the Curtis Bay boat yard. On their first visit, they were escorted to a covered work bay and got their first look at their new vessel.

Bear said, "That is one ugly boat."

Meeting them was Ensign Robert Ferguson, "Hello fellows. Are you the new owners of this pile of bones? I am in charge of the renovation. Welcome."

Jack shook his hand and responded, "Yes, I understand that you know how to do magic on old heaps of junk."

"Yes, we are well on our way. Let's walk around and I'll show you what we are doing.

"The metal deck was removed almost the first day. You can see that we made the inside sparkle. It is even better than it was new."

From there, they looked down at the installed new engines and drivetrains. They were massive. Taking up almost a quarter of the engine room was a two-thousand-gallon diesel fuel tank.

Ensign Ferguson jokingly remarked, "Hope you guys have big limits on your credit card when you go to the filling station."

Bear pointed at a large pump attached to the starboard engine, "What is that?"

"It's the hydraulic pump. It needs to be that large as it will power all the controls for the stealth conversion."

"I have been very curious about how that's going to work. Have you finalized the plans?"

"The idea was proven in our test model. It is still a work in progress. We call it Auto Camo."

"Explain."

"The first part was the sides of the hull. Above the waterline the base paint will be black and jungle camo. Then, on each side, we will add a line of old tires mounted on a half-inch thick aluminum plate. Think of tires installed on a garage door and painted like the junk salvage boat. In the down position it looks like a worn out workboat. In the up position, the tires and mount are hinged along the top edge of the sides of the ship or properly called the gunwale. Anyway, the tires and mount will swing out and over the gunwale. In doing so, it will expose the camo paint. The tires will continue moving over to the inside of the gunwale and stored out of sight."

"That is simple. Awesome. What about the tower?"

"Well, let's separate the bridge where the controls, wheel, and electronics are mounted. Consider it as the top floor of the fifteen-foot tower. The bridge is not involved with the conversion process."

"Okay, I can see that."

"The Bridge will have bulletproof glass and black metal trim and will not change during Auto Camo conversion. It's the sides of the tower that must change and you won't believe the way we are going to do the magic."

"I can't imagine how you are going to do that."

"Have you seen advertising signs or billboards along the highway that change the message by rotating slats? Sort of like a window shade that you can open or close the blinds by twisting a handle?"

"Yes."

"Another example is window shutters. You can close shutters by moving one blade of the shutter and the others follow, from open to close."

"Yeah, I'm beginning to get your idea."

"Well, think of long aluminum slats or planks about six inches in width and maybe eight feet tall. They will be vertically mounted, side-by-side, on pivots that will allow them to rotate. They will be mechanically linked with gears to turn in unison, like shutters. On one side we will paint them to look like a dirty old workboat with the name of your salvage company on it and on the other we'll paint it to look like a military attack boat painted in jungle camo. The slats are linked together and powered by hydraulic motors. Oh , by the way, the slats will have an interlocking edge that will form a rigid wall. This arrangement should withstand gale force winds."

"I cannot wait to see that work."

"We should have it done by the next time you visit. By the way, we begin painting in a week. We need the name of the boat as a salvage ship and the name of the camo boat. The name must change to maintain the disguise."

"Oh, I thought they told you. The name of the company is *Sanford Salvage and Water Repai*rs. The name of that boat is *Castaway* and the name of the camo boat is *Revenge*.

"I like it. We are going to have fun with this one."

"By the way," Jack asked, "Have you talked to anyone about the weapons to be placed on the boat?"

"Yes, I have a list here from our armory. Let me see..." The Ensign flipped through the paperwork on his clipboard. "Oh, here it is. Whoa, you are going to like this! We will be installing two fifty-caliber M2 Browning machine guns. One mounted on the bow and one on the stern. They have a rate of fire of five hundred rounds per minute and have a range of reaching targets over fifteen hundred yards. The machine guns will have a custom cover, designed to look like a winch or small crane that belongs to the salvage boat. To use them, just unzip the cover and it's ready to go. Also on board will be various handguns and three M4 Assault Rifles with a rate of fire of six hundred rounds per minute in the automatic mode, plus two assault twelve-gauge shotguns."

Both Jack and Bear smiled and shook their heads.

"We have a lot to do, but it will be ready for pick up when you finish your training. My security clearance allowed me to be privy to the use of this beast. It sounds like a needed project. Good luck and good hunting. We have a lot of bad guys out there."

Chapter 19

At a local seafood restaurant near the shipyard, Captain Brad McCormick, Ensign Robert Ferguson, Jack, and Bear were celebrating the end of training. Shortly after being seated, the Captain asked the waiter to bring four of the coldest beers in the house.

"That would be Samuel Adams," the waiter replied.

"Good choice, I have developed a taste for that one," Bear added.

The beers arrived and the Captain held his mug up high, "Good work gentlemen. Our project is off to a great start."

"Cheers," they all shouted.

"Robert tells me they are ready for your ship's sea trials. I hope it floats," the Captain said.

"I think you will be impressed," replied Robert. "I'll bet it will hit almost fifty knots."

They all chose the house special of a steamed shellfish sampling that was poured out in the middle of the table on newspapers. Each had a small bowl of melted butter, lobster crackers, and seafood forks. They would reach in and take any item they wanted. It was messy but delicious. An hour and a half later, they agreed to meet at the docks at zero-eight-hundred to do a walkthrough.

Later on the stroll back to their hotel, Bear said, "I think I am going to like our new lifestyle."

"Don't get used to it. We're heading back to the Swordfish. Marge is a good cook, but she doesn't hold a candle to this."

The next morning, the boys found quite a crowd standing around the *Castaway*. Joining Captain McCormick and Ensign Ferguson was a naval architect, a mechanical engineer, a drivetrain engineer, and an electronics technician.

Ferguson announced to all, "Before we leave the docks, you might want to visit the restrooms here, we did not have time to add a head."

"Oh well," the tech said, "it won't be the first time we've peed over the stern."

Jack looked at Bear, "We need to do something about that before we leave for the Swordfish."

As they all came aboard, the engineer and drivetrain guy went down to the engine room and the others went up to the bridge where the tech began checking each part of the electronics package. After the okay from preliminary checks, the signal was given to start the engines. As each came alive, a deep-throated rumble caused a smile on everyone. Ensign Ferguson pointed out that the noise level wasn't as bad as he expected, but that the engine room would be very loud.

"We put in a lot of soundproofing before we installed the engines."

After five minutes, the drivetrain engineer reported the visual checks were normal and he felt no vibration, it was good to go. Jack expertly navigated the boat into the harbor and was out to the jetties in another thirty minutes.

"Crank it up to half throttle," ordered the naval architect. Castaway responded like a sports car, was easily cutting through the surf and began to point her nose slightly in the air as the speed increased to twenty-five knots. "Looking good, now take a few small turns."

Jack followed the instructions.

"No problem so far. Full speed now."

The noise level rose considerably and the guys in the engine room put on maximum hearing protection. They were carefully monitoring for any out-of-normal conditions.

They reported, "Everything seems okay. Oil pressures normal, temperature normal, no vibrations. Nice and stable."

"Looks like we are maxing out at forty-eight knots. Probably hit over fifty in calm seas. Okay everyone, hold on for a max turn at full speed. Okay Jack, now turn."

The boat started to lean into the turn and at the maximum, the rails were almost in the water. It was stressed, but structurally it held together.

"Now straighten out and idle down."

Jack did as he was asked. The boat came to the normal position and was floating in the waves like a buoy marker.

"All hands spread out to look for damage and report back."

The search took ten minutes and all reports came back as normal. The naval architect announced that the ship looked sound to him and told Captain McCormick that he judged the *Castaway* to be seaworthy. The drivetrain engineer also reported that he could not detect any problems.

"One last test and then we will cruise around for a few hours to check for long-term leaks or problems. If there are none, we can call it a day."

"What's the last test?" asked Jack.

"It will be two tests in one. The electronics and your ability to use them."

"What do you want me to do?"

"Here are two coordinates. When you navigate to the first, turn to the other. When you reach it, stop the boat."

"That sounds easy."

"Maybe not. I am going to simulate a storm blackout by placing a black curtain around you and the electronics. Let me point out, we have boat traffic out here. Don't hit anyone. Are you ready?"

"I guess so. Let's do it."

He had done this before, but it was a simulation in class, this seemed a lot more difficult. The Captain and Ensign Ferguson assembled the curtain and said, "Go, you are on your own."

At first, Jack was scared and nervous, but soon he settled down when he realized it was just like the simulator. If the radar and navigation were working correctly, he would be fine. First, he looked at the radar display and could see four objects either in front of him or on the sides. Looking again, two were stationary and two were moving, but none were currently a problem. As he approached the first mark and made his turn, he saw that one of the boats was now on a collision course. He adjusted and veered so that the vessel would pass on the port side with ample clearance. When the radar indicated he had safely cleared, he fixed his new course to the second mark and stopped within twenty-five yards of his target.

"Did we pass?" asked Jack.

"Good on both counts," answered the Captain. "Give the controls to Bear and we will begin to cruise around for a while."

Bear looked around and worriedly asked the Captain, "Is it also a storm blackout simulation?"

"No, we don't need to do that again. We're good."

They were back at the docks by mid-afternoon and the boys went straight to the camping store to buy everything needed to get them prepared for the trip. They thought, *We just need to get home the best we can and then we can fix up the inside of the cabin.*

The list included two cots and sleeping bags, two folding chairs, a folding table, a Coleman stove, cooking utensils, three large ice chests, and various other small items. The must-buy item was a portable five-gallon toilet and chemicals. On their way back, they also stopped at a grocery store and bought water, paper, canned food, and supplies.

During breakfast at the hotel the next morning, Jack whispered, "Today will be exciting. We get to play with the fifty-caliber machine guns."

"Yeah, then we are off to screw up some bad guys."

"Exactly."

"Let's get to the docks a little early so we can load in our new gear."

"Ya' know we need to find a way to anchor the toilet. We sure don't want that crap getting spilled when it gets rough out there."

"I think I saw some angle iron laying around the shipyard. Maybe we can get it welded to the floor and make a cradle for it."

While they were getting that done, the Coast Guard gang arrived and stepped aboard to see what they were welding. Noticing the toilet, Ferguson said, "Oh, I see. Good thinking."

The Captain then said, "We are all here for today's trials."

"We are ready when you are," responded Bear.

"Take us out. Here are the coordinates. Earlier this morning, we towed a scrapped barge to this location. It will become an artificial reef. Fish love old sunken things. They have anchored it there for us to put it full of holes and sink it. Sounds like fun, huh?"

"Yes sir," snapped Bear.

"Sir? Did you refer to me as Sir? Well I see something must have rubbed off on you from boot camp."

"Yeah, I just loved Chief Weatherford."

After a little over an hour, Captain McCormick said, "Let's stop here to make the camo conversion. Then we will move on to the barge."

Jack pulled the throttle to idle and Bear reached over to the control board and found the hinged plastic cap labeled "Hull Conversion". He flipped the top and pushed the button. Everyone watched as the hydraulic motor lifts worked flawlessly. In less than a minute, the tires were tucked neatly against the insides of the gunwale. Bear stayed inside the bridge while the others filed out to the deck to watch the transformation of the tower. Pushing the "Tower Conversion" button caused the paneling to begin to rotate to the camo side, again taking less than a minute.

"That was amazing! Good job Ensign Ferguson," the Captain shouted. The mechanical engineer was as proud as if he just became a new father.

Before testing the weapons, the electronics tech mentioned, "This would be a good time to try out the com gear. Included with the com package for the boat are four radio sets which allowed hands-free radio communications with everyone on the boat plus the Coast Guard."

The tech helped Jack, Bear, and the Captain to adjust each set for a proper fit and to get ready for the operational test. It consisted of a small receiver worn in a pocket, an earpiece, and a lapel lip mic. After a very short training session, they were ready to begin. Jacked walked to the bow and unzipped the cover of the machine gun while the Ensign did the same to the rear mount.

"We are now fully ready for action and it took less than five minutes total."

The Captain climbed back to the bridge and shouted down, "I'll drive this bad boy. You guys get ready. Use the M4 Assault Rifles first. That old rust bucket won't last long with the machine guns.

He pulled up to within fifty yards from the barge and over the com set he said, "Write your initials on the side of the barge."

Both Bear and Jack got the hang of it very quickly, even adjusting for movement of the waves. The assault rifles were light and accurate.

"Now, let's hit it with the fifty-calibers. Keep shooting until you sink the old tub."

Immediately, noise, smoke, and vibration came over the boat. The barge began to look like Swiss cheese. It tilted over and began to roll away from them. The shooting stopped and they watched as the barge slowly began to sink then went faster as it filled with sea water.

The Captain looked down from the bridge and spoke into his com set, "Looks like everything is working just fine. What do ya think?"

"I can't believe it!" responded the boys over the com sets.

"I guess that does it. Let's go back to the docks and pen this beast up for the day."

As they were leaving, the naval architect called for a quick meeting.

"Gentlemen, fundamentally you have a very sound boat here, especially considering its mission, but I am concerned about the tires. They would normally be fine, but if you get into gale force winds and associated waves the tires may restrict the control of the ship, maybe even be ripped off and cause damage. I suggest if you have severe weather, change to the camo setup for the hull and the tires will be out of the way."

"Good point. We did not think of that, but you are correct," the Captain answered. "The camo solution would work but it sort of blows our cover. So guys, as you come into shore and slow down be sure to put it back to the junky mode. Okay boys, looks like this is it. You are on your own. You will have maybe a two-week trip back home, depending on how many stops you make. Here is a list of some of the Coast Guard stations on the way back. The Captains of each station knows what we're doing and is very interested. They will welcome you to stay there for a night or two. Don't let them talk to you into showing the Auto Camo while docked. If they want to see it work, you must take them out to sea and away from non-secure eyes. As you leave in the morning, stop by our fueling station and get your tank topped off. I guess that does it. Good luck and safe sailing."

Jack and Bear shook everyone's hands and extended their thanks for the trust given to them, "We will make you proud."

The Captain remembered, "Be sure to stop at our facility back in Houston. We are sending you a truckload of ammunition for your use. You will need to store it in a secure location. What kind of pistols have you selected?"

Bear answered, "45 caliber".

Jack said, "9 millimeter".

"See you in Houston."

Part Six –

Looking for a Luau -

The Return Home

Chapter 20

With Jack's new Coast Guard Captains Credentials, he was extremely cautious in piloting their daily routes. The last thing he wanted was to put the boat in a lousy situation that required the Coast Guard to come bail him out. He thought, *Nice and comfortable. Keep it simple.*

"Bear," he said, "I want to ease into this trip and not get in over our heads. We are going to stay within five miles of shoreline for the first few days."

"Where are we headed tonight?" asked Bear.

"It should be an easy ten-hour run down to Virginia Beach to the Little Creek Coast Guard Station. Captain Gill Roberts has reserved a space for us, sounds like a nice guy. We can use the showers. He wants to take us out to eat and see what we are all about."

"Hope it is not too formal," Bear replied. "I left my tuxedo back at the Swordfish."

"Oh, he knows what to expect."

The trip down was stress-free and as they entered the harbor it was evident that this was a big Navy town. It seemed that the ships were stacked in like sardines. The streets were full of young, enlisted men and officers enjoying the evening at the many bars and restaurants around the harbor.

Captain Roberts was a small man with a big baritone voice. He was a happy man, full of funny stories of the Coast Guard. His historical knowledge of the beginning days of the country and Virginia Beach's ties to the first Navy were entertaining. Near the end of the meal, he began to talk about the seriousness of the illegal narcotics industry and of course that brought up the new MSST program.

"Yes, Captain McCormick recruited us for the Marine Safety and Security Team. We are delighted to be the prototype for this program," said Jack.

Roberts responded, "If we can make this work, it will give us a tremendous advantage in apprehending the scum criminals that walk our streets."

Bear said, "We are looking forward to it. Thank you for your hospitality."

"Well, maybe when you are complete with your work here you could join the Coast Guard,"

"No thanks, I don't think I want to meet Chief Weatherford again."

They all laughed and exited the restaurant

Jack whispered to Bear, "Dude, I thought you liked Chief Weatherford."

"Ya know, you always have fond memories of your first Drill Sergeant. What an ass."

The next port on the schedule was Charleston, South Carolina located three hundred miles south of Virginia Beach. Jack calculated that this should be a sixteen-hour trip and they would experience their first overnight voyage. He estimated that they should arrive early the next morning. After eight hours, he checked their progress with the navigation electronics and found they were not even close to being half-way.

"Hey Bear, something is not right. Take the wheel for a while. I need to do some more checking." Jack stepped over to the navigation table to check the charts and consult the pilot's book. "Oh, that's it. Bear, I made a mistake. I forgot about the Gulf Stream."

"What's that?"

"It explains it here… 'The Gulf Stream is a warm Atlantic Ocean current that originates in the Gulf of Mexico and stretches to the tip of Florida and then flows North following the

Eastern coastlines of the United States and Canada. It is typically sixty miles wide and three thousand feet deep. The current velocity is fastest near the surface, with the maximum speed typical of five knots.'"

"What does that mean?"

"Simply put, we are moving through the water at twenty knots, but the water is coming into us at five knots. Twenty minus five is fifteen. That means we are moving toward our target at fifteen knots and instead of getting into Charleston early in the morning, we will get there about noon. Not a problem."

For the overnight trip, Jack and Bear set up a sleep rotation of two hours. It wasn't much to it. Just to keep the ship pointed to the next navigation mark and to monitor the radar for problems. If there was anything out of the ordinary and one would wake the other. They were both awake at sun-up and enjoyed the morning at sea. Pulling into the Coast Guard station was not a hassle as the station captain had arranged a slip for *Castaway* and an eager young Ensign was there to help.

He sharply saluted as he said, "Welcome to Charleston. May I be of some assistance?"

"Thanks, but no thanks. We don't have much luggage, but we would like to use your bathroom and shower facilities."

Pointing to the building, he said, "It's just down the hall and on the right. By the way, the Captain is away at a meeting with the Navy. He wishes to apologize to you for not being here."

"Not a problem. We are just on our way to our home base in South Texas. We will be leaving in the morning."

"If you need anything else, I will be in the office."

"I am sure we will be fine but thank you."

A good shower and a nap were all they needed to venture out to see the sights of historic Charleston.

Bear said, "I read that this is where Blackbeard the pirate lived."

"Well, let's go find out."

The tourist industry has made much of the glamorous life of the pirate and the boys were eager to jump in and enjoy the fantasies. They found many stores which sold items of the pirate lore and some great costumes. One eatery of interest was the Pirate House. It once was a boarding house, gambling den, and trade center for contraband goods. Some even believed that it had a secret tunnel which led from the basement to provide access to the ships and was used to kidnap young men and either force them to join the ways of the pirate or die.

They made it back to the *Castaway* with three different pirate costumes and a giant pirate flag. Bear reminded Jack that they had become the masters of disguise and they could create their characters, "Why not pirates?"

With a pause for laughter, Jack said, "Next stop, Miami."

Remembering to calculate the effects of the Gulf Stream, the estimated time of arrival was still off by an hour. Jack was surprised by the amount of traffic that it did not allow him to take the most efficient course to the Miami Coast Guard Station. Even so, they were securely docked and ready for the showers by sixteen-hundred hours. The lieutenant who was assigned to welcome them was as professional and helpful, as usual.

Before leaving, he said, "Captain Greta Malkovich asked you to stop by her office to have a few words with her. I think she wants to remind you how easy it is to end up in the wrong place. Miami can be very dangerous. For your information, she is a strict, by-the-book station officer and is also very opinionated. Be prepared for anything. Good luck."

After showering and putting on their best clothes, Jack and Bear opened her office door and found a desk clerk smiling at them, "May I help you?"

"We are here to see Captain Malkovich, I believe that she wanted to see us."

"Yes, she and Officer Dan Sanchez of the DEA are waiting for you. I will announce you."

Greta was okay to start with but it went downhill quickly. "Welcome to Miami. Captain Brad McCormick has some very nice things to say about you two. Please meet Steve Ortega of the DEA, the task force leader for drug enforcement in Dade County."

Everyone shook hands, said their hellos, and sat down.

"Just for the record," Captain Malkovich said, "I was the only one who voted no on the Marine Safety Security Team or the MSST Program and I especially did not like the idea of a contractor program. Now, after seeing you two snotty nosed kids parade around like some bad-ass enforcement dudes, I am going to call again to voice my displeasure."

"Sorry about that Captain," said Jack, "but we are not in enforcement. We will be your advanced eyes to give you a heads up for the opportunity of a drug bust."

"I don't give a shit what you think. All I know is that it will be the Coast Guard coming out to save your asses. You will cost us resources, time, and budget expenses to keep you safe. I would rather spend that same money trying to reduce Norco crime in Miami."

Jack sat straight up and said, "We are not here to change your mind, so Bear and I will get out of your way and leave you alone as soon as possible. We can leave tonight if you like."

"Not so fast. I haven't finished yet. You have no idea how dangerous these guys are. You are severely under-gunned and I don't care how fast your boat is, they have a faster one. If they think you are out to hurt them, they will kill you."

"Again," Jack said, "we are not here to change your mind. Can we go now?"

"No, I am trying to save your lives. One more thing, in a few hours Steve Ortega and the SWAT team from Miami Vice will be out enforcing arrest warrants for some of these characters. I want you to ride along with Steve here, just to see what you are fighting. After tonight, and if you still want to do the program, you are free to go. I cannot stop you."

Ortega spoke up and said, "I will pick you up in a couple of hours. You will be riding with me. If you have a bulletproof vest, wear it."

"Yeah, we have them. See you in a little while."

After a hamburger at McDonald's, the boys met Steve Ortega in the Coast Guard parking lot. Both were wearing a military vest under the beach shirts.

As the car came to a stop, Ortega said, "This is Judge Kelly, he is also observing in case he needs to modify the warrant. You guys sit in the back, me and the judge will sit up here. We will be there in about twenty minutes."

Bear noticed the police had begun to block any access to the neighborhood.

Ortega pointed to the roadblocks and said, "We don't want any armed support group coming in to help the target. By the way, he is the boss-man for the west side dealers and he has broken his parole agreement. We will be taking him back to jail and he's not going to like that. He will be armed and dangerous."

"Does he know that we're coming?"

"I am sure he does. As soon as we put up the barricades, he probably got a phone call."

"Doesn't he care that he may be shot dead?"

"Yeah, it's the risk he takes. Plus he thinks he has supernatural powers. Thinks he can maybe kill a few cops and we'll just throw him back in jail. You're not going to believe the balls that they have and if you think these guys are bad, you won't believe what organized crime has become. The Mafia has access to military weapons and enough money to buy off the local politicians and even some of the cops." Ortega reached into the glove box and pulled out a small radio receiver, "Turn this on during the takedown. You can hear the police communication as it takes place. It's almost like you are there."

The police cruiser eased up a street and parked across from the target house. A radio check confirmed that everyone was in place and had the house surrounded. A SWAT van pulled into the driveway and parked as eight cops in full protective gear positioned themselves at various locations around the yard.

With the 'Go' command, a very loud speaker from the van announced, "We are here to pick up Juan Magill Cortez. Come out with your hands up or we will use force."

The cop repeated the warning in Spanish.

Moments later, the front door opened and a woman walked out with her hands in the air. Someone from the inside reached around and closed the door behind her. Ortega got out of the car and walked to the front lawn along with a SWAT officer. She was crying when she talked to the officer and he escorted her to the van.

Ortega walked across the street and said to the judge, "She wants to know what kind of deal she can make for her husband."

"Tell her that we will not shoot if her husband surrenders unarmed and with his hands up."

Ortega walked back to the van and handed the wife the microphone, "You tell him."

The wife asked, "Can I go back inside to tell him?"

"No, you are staying here."

A few minutes later, the door opened. Cortez came out with a gun in one hand and a baby in the other. He shouted, "Give my wife the keys to a police car or I will kill the baby."

Ortega whispered to the SWAT leader, "Are your snipers in place?"

"Yes."

"Okay. Pull up a cruiser to the curb. Get out of the car and give her the keys. We have snipers in three directions, so he cannot hide behind the baby from them all. As soon as you have a clear shot to the head, take it. Do not let him in the car.

"Roger."

The shot was clean, the baby and wife were safe, and another bad guy was now off the street.

On the way back to the Coast Guard Station, Jack asked, "How often does this happen?"

"Not enough and even at that as soon as we get rid of one, another one pops up. It is a big business."

"This one seemed pretty clean. Are all confrontations like that?"

"No, about half the time a gun battle breaks out and frequently more than one gets killed."

"How safe is it for the officers?"

"This is the most dangerous activity a police officer faces. An officer is wounded about ten percent of the time in a gun battle, but very rarely is it deadly."

Bear commented, "The way I see it is, if we do our job and you and the Coast Guard can block the drugs from entering the US, there would be less reason for these crimes to even exist."

"Where there is a demand, they will always find a way but I like your attitude."

The next morning, as the boys were filling their water jugs and tidying up the boat for the open water. Bear looked over at Jack and chuckled, "Do you know who Greta Malkovich reminds me of?"

Jack stopped, "Well, tell me."

"A fat, ugly Chief Weatherford with a bun tied so tight that his eyes squint."

"Come on Bear, get Chief Weatherford out of your mind. I can't take it anymore. I'm getting tired of laughing."

Chapter 21

NOWA issued a marine warning as Jack and Bear rose before sunup. They had planned to make a two-day trip around the tip of Florida and across the Gulf of Mexico.

After considering the weather, he said to Bear, "Looks like we have three options. One is to stay here and wait for better weather. Another is plow through the rough seas and head straight to New Orleans or we can get around the tip and find a safe spot somewhere around Tampa. What do you think?"

"How bad is the storm?"

"Not too bad right now. It is between Cuba and Mexico, but it is forecast to build into gale force winds of forty knots from the southwest with severe ten-foot waves. It is pretty dangerous. We would get beat up pretty badly."

Bear considered the situation and replied, "The thought of even seeing Greta Malkovich rules out staying here.

"Really? You don't like Miami?"

"Not much, I do like the good-looking girls, and especially Key Lime Pie, but that's about it. No reason to stay. Let's go to Tampa."

"Agreed, but that is still a twelve hour trip in good weather. By that time, we will be getting hit."

"I am not staying here! Chalk it up as a storm sailing experience. Let's go now and get a jump on it."

They were motoring out of the Miami harbor with enough light to see and cruising south at twenty-five knots and eight miles from shore, as they made a sweeping turn past Key West, the weather began to get angry quickly. Jack stopped the boat to change the configuration of the tires to the Camo position and securely stored them inside of the gunwales and out of the wind.

Bring it on, he thought.

By noon the winds were pushing *Castaway* into the Florida coast, forcing them to take a more northwesterly line. The swells were now growing to four-foot waves from the top to the troughs. Jack was forced to slow their speed to make a smoother ride.

Two more hours of pounding caused Jack to say, "Take over the wheel and keep us on this compass point. I need to find a closer shelter. I am not in the mood to put up with this crap if it is not necessary."

After a few minutes and a radio phone call, Jack shouted out to Bear, "Found it. Fort Myer is directly downwind from here and we should be there in about two hours. I called the Coast Guard station there and they are reserving us overnight parking."

Another hour passed and the force of the winds and wave heights increased. Jack looked like he was having fun and Bear asked, "Where did you learn how to steer a boat like this? I would be scared shitless."

"We studied it at the Coast Guard's Captain School but I learned the technique at Vail."

"Did you say Vail? Like in Vail, Colorado?"

"Yes, it's just like skiing a downhill course with a bunch of moguls."

"Vail? You know how to ski?"

"Oh, I must have never told you of my boyhood days. My family spent the winters at Vail and the summers at South Padre. Dad was a ski instructor and I was skiing before I was five."

"What does that have to do with it?"

"A mogul is a mound of snow. When you find one, you will generally find a lot of them. Think of the mogul as a wave. Now, if I am skiing downhill and see a mogul field, I must not just run straight over the top and straight down to the next one. I would crash right into the new mogul face first. The proper way to handle a mogul field is first to slow down. Secondly, don't go over the top straight on. The key is, at the top, angle off at about forty-five degrees to the left or the right. Then you will set up for the next one and repeat the sequence. You go up, turn near the top, and straighten back up to climb the next mogul. You can get into a rhythm. It's fun."

"Okay, how do you make a turn? Say the ski run turns left."

"Easy, if you want to turn left, make all left turns off the top of the moguls. Alternating the turns will cause you to go straight. Make a left, next make a right, and next make a left."

"Well, it seems to work for you."

"Yeah, Fort Myers is somewhat to the left from here. Watch me. I will go straight into the swell and as I get almost on top of it, I will turn the boat left at about forty-five degrees and scoot down to the trough. Then turn back into the wave and do it again.

"Amazing, now I can say that I know how to ski."

"I don't think so."

As *Castaway* approached the coastline, Jack adjusted the direction to match the center opening of the jetties. Once inside the barriers, the waters calmed but the wind was still howling. Shortly, and with a little help, they were tucked snugly into the Coast Guard station's protected docks.

"Come in and dry off," the Coast Guardsman shouted. "Bring some dry clothes. We have hot showers and a lounge with a big screen T.V."

The boys shut down the boat, picked up their duffle bags, and ran to the station. There, as the Guardsman took off his yellow rain slicker, Jack said, "Thanks for the help. It's pretty bad out there. My name is Jack Mahan and this is Bear DeMarco."

"Yeah, I know who you are. You guys have made quite a name for yourselves already. My name is Lieutenant Danny Miller. I am the station chief here. Please just call me Danny."

"We'll take you up on your kind offer. We haven't finished the inside of the boat yet. It doesn't even have a head or running water. We will correct that when we get back to Texas."

"Hey, there is a pizza place across the street. While you guys are getting fixed up, I will bring us a couple of large pepperonis. I'll bet you're hungry."

Bear put on his biggest smile and said, "Super, I can smell it now."

Over the pizza, a friendship began to develop. During the conversation, the boys were surprised to learn that Danny Miller was the youngest station chief in Coast Guard history, just twenty-six. He grew up in San Diego and joined the Coast Guard after getting a degree in Math from UCLA. He advanced quickly at various locations and was stationed in Fort Myers when the current station chief retired.

Danny knew quite a lot about Jack and Bear through the Coast Guard's private chat network. He said, "I would have loved to be a contractor in the new MSST, but there was no way could I have arranged the financing. I will be following you each step of the way. If you guys need anything along the way, call me."

The conversation continued and a stable bond of friendship developed. Bear said, "We are on a quest for finding a luau, any suggestions?"

"As a matter of fact, Ft. Myers is holding its annual pig roast contest this weekend. Most of the city and the boating community show up. Weather should have cleared by then. It is always a blast." Continuing Danny said, "Shops will be setting up tents and we will have about ten bands starting at noon and lasting through midnight. Also, if you are interested, we will have a beach volleyball tournament going on most of the day. You guys just gotta stay. Better still, I am dating this nurse and I will have her bring a couple of friends. Never hurts to have a female companion at a pig roast."

Jack jumped in, "We need to wait out the storm anyway. Why not? Sounds like fun."

Bear also responded, "I need to change the fluids and filters in the new engines and drivetrains. It will be a good time to do that. By the way, can I borrow a few tools?"

"Sure. Maybe I could get you to look at a problem with one of my cruisers. We are having trouble with shifting. It wants to pop back into neutral."

"Be glad to, I will do that first."

By the end of the next day, Bear had completed his tasks and he and Jack were watching sports on the big screen T.V. when Danny walked in.

"You guys are in luck, my girlfriend is bringing a couple of nurses with her to the pig roast. I have met them and I think you will be pleased."

Bear said, "I fixed your cruiser. It was a linkage problem. Just needed some adjustments."

"Great. You guys make yourself at home. I have to attend a meeting in Miami tonight. I'll be back tomorrow for the pig roast. If you need anything, just ask one of my guys."

"Bear said, "Give our regards to Greta Malkovich."

Danny made it back to the station a little before noon.

"You guys ready for a pig roast? It's co-sponsored by the Coast Guard, so I need to change into my uniform. We will be taking a rigid inflatable boat to the beach. Be ready to leave in fifteen minutes."

They pulled into the cove and docked near the big tent area. The contestants were already preparing their secret pig recipes and had the grills hot and cooking. Scattered around the big tent were several smaller tents set up to sell their wares, tee shirts were the most popular. On the stage, the first band was warming up with the island sounds of a steel drum.

Danny was looking around and suddenly said, "Ahh, there they are!" He waved.

Jack and Bear were stunned as three gorgeous girls walked up wearing bikinis, sun tops, and hats. Danny kissed his girl and said, "Ladies, these are my new friends. Meet Jack Mahan and Bear DeMarco. Guys meet my girlfriend Liz and her friends Kate and Jinny."

After a few awkward moments, all of them went over to the beer stand and selected a Corona with a lime slice tucked into the tab. Kate was at least six feet tall, very curvy, and naturally attracted to Bear. Jinny then matched up with Jack. They all walked over to the spectator section and selected a picnic table that offered a good view of the bands and the beach.

It seemed that all were getting along well and spent the afternoon sharing stories about nursing and sailing. Later in the evening, Danny was asked to be one of the judges for the cook-off. He laughed and said that he was qualified as he was a natural ham.

Jack responded with, "Danny that was so bad."

All of them laughed, lifted their beers, and gave Danny a toast.

Later Danny urged the table to help him select the best pork and they all enjoyed testing each contestant's offering.

Danny crowned the cook-off champion and as he came back to the table he noticed that Bear and Kate had disappeared. He looked at Jack and asked, "Where did they go?"

The girls giggled and said, "Oh, she had enough sun and wanted to show Bear some more of the city. I doubt that they'll come back."

They listened to the bands for a while and around ten, Jinny announced that she had an early shift the next morning. She said her goodbye to Jack and asked if Liz wanted a ride.

"No thanks, I'll take the boat back with the boys and Danny can take me home from there."

"Okay then. Thanks guys, I had a nice time."

After she left, Danny kidded Jack, "What did you do to piss her off?"

"Oh, she asked me what I do for a living."

"And what did you tell her?"

"The truth. I said that I had two jobs, one on a salvage boat and the other as a professional beachcomber. I think she was looking for something with a little more stability."

Everyone had a good laugh and listened to another band.

Bear did not come home that night and the next morning he dragged himself in with a smile on his face. He looked at both Danny and Jack and said, "Why are you staring? I had to stay. She promised to fix me breakfast."

Jack stuck around the air-conditioned lounge watching a baseball talk show and talking with Danny. Bear showered, changed clothes, and two hours later Kate picked him up to go exploring. Like the day before, Jack didn't see him again until just before they were scheduled to leave. The storms were gone and seas were calm. New Orleans was about twenty-six hours away.

Danny followed them out of the harbor and into the open water to avoid any curious eyes. He wanted to see the transformation demonstration. As he watched the boat go from a salvage boat to a deadly military craft, he fired off his siren and waved goodbye to his new friends.

As they were leaving, Bear slapped a big hand on Jack's back and said, "Now, that's what I call a luau."

"Yep, the best Coast Guard station we have visited."

Losing sight of land, Jack looked over at Bear and said, "What's wrong with you? You haven't mentioned Greta Malkovich in a long time."

Bear's response was, "Greta who? Don't think I know her" and then turned his attention back to the sea with a smile on his face.

Chapter 22

With flat seas, winds at ten knots, only a few clouds, and temperatures not reaching above ninety, the weather and the gulf waters were spectacular that day. Jack had plotted a course to a northwest compass point. New Orleans was five-hundred-fifty miles. Cruising at thirty-five knots during the day and twenty knots at night should put them at the Coast Guard docks and put up by mid- to late morning. Their primary concern was keeping a sharp eye on the radar to watch for other vessels and off-shore oil and gas platforms. They were surprised to notice that not all of the platforms were listed on their latest charts, but had comfort in knowing the radar would always point them out. Also, they had to be on the watch for floating debris that the radar would not pick up. In rough seas, like the week before, sometimes a freighter might lose a few containers. Hitting one at thirty knots could do a lot of damage to a ship the size of *Castaway*.

They passed the day singing, joking, and planning the modifications they would do when they reach the Swordfish. They had plenty of money left over from the initial investment plus the incoming monthly contract fees. They decided not to go first class on the living quarters just yet, but they did list their must-have priorities. On the top were plumbing, electrical, and a super big air-conditioning system. These would become the foundation for the future improvements. They could always upgrade the furnishings later.

That night they used the rotating shift schedule which had worked before. Because of the excellent weather, each was able to sleep, which resulted in being rested and wide awake the next morning.

The New Orleans Coast Guard station was one of the largest they had seen. It not only had responsibility for the local Gulf of Mexico traffic, but was also in charge of monitoring all shipping either entering or exiting the Mississippi River. This location had a staff of over two hundred. Captain Joseph Alsop was the officer-in-charge. However, most of his time was spent in Washington. Commander Melvin Dickinson was second-in-command and was on duty when *Castaway* arrived.

A very jolly lieutenant jogged up to help with the lines as Jack began to back into the slip. Once secure and the engines stopped, the Guardsman shouted up, "Welcome to New Orleans. We were expecting you. My name is Jones, but everyone around here calls me 'Boss Man'. I am to take you upstairs to introduce you to the Commander."

"Thanks," said Jack.

"The acting station commander is anxious to meet you. Please bring your duffels and I'll take you to his office."

On the way, Bear asked, "Anything special going on in this fair city?"

"Mr. DeMarco, there is always something going on in New Orleans. We have a professional basketball game tomorrow night. You guys like the Pelicans?"

"Not my team. What else ya got?"

"You are in luck. We have a movie premiere tonight in the Super Dome."

"Now, that sounds interesting. What movie?"

The new *Mad Max* movie. It is going to be more like a carnival. They will have a lot of booths selling franchised stuff. You can get autographed posters. Most the attendees will be dressed out in their versions of *Mad Max* costumes. When the movie starts, they will show it on the big scoreboard."

"Now that sounds like fun. Is it open to the public?"

The lieutenant smiled the biggest smile Bear had ever seen and said, "Sold out, but I can get you a couple of tickets for the right price. My brother is a scalper but I can get ya a deal. That's why they call me the Boss Man."

"How much?"

"Fifty each."

Bear looked at Jack to get an agreement and replied, "Deal."

"And for that price, I can get you two tickets to the best jazz house on Bourbon Street."

"Great, I like jazz. Who's playing tonight?"

The Boss Man smiled again and said, "It's never a band. It's several musicians who just show up to play. My other brother owns the place. I think you'll enjoy spending some time there. The good stuff doesn't get started until after ten. Just mention the Boss Man sent you. That will get you good seats."

Jack added, "And do you have a recommendation for a nice place to eat?"

"This is New Orleans man, home of some of the best meals in the world. Just walk down Bourbon or Royal streets. Anyplace with white tablecloths will be great."

"Well, here we are at the station office. Let me introduce you."

"Thanks Lieutenant."

"Come see me when you're through here and I'll show you the rooms and showers. I'll get my brother to send me the tickets."

As they walked through the door, Commander Melvin Dickinson stood to extend his hand and warmly welcomed Jack and Bear. "I hope the Boss Man here has taken care of you. I am happy you stopped In New Orleans, as I am very interested in the MSST Program. You guys have a real challenge ahead of you."

"Thank you sir. We plan to make the Coast Guard proud."

"I know that we are concentrating on the drug problem right now, but we are also facing another large and growing illegal activity that has me deeply concerned, human trafficking."

Jack looked thoughtful and troubled, "Really, I wasn't aware of it being that big of a problem."

"The media has not given it a lot of attention, but in economic terms it is almost on the same scale as the drug industry. Selling human beings is slavery, yet still today it is a huge business. Soon the Coast Guard will be charged to end it. It is just as wrong as the drug business."

"Tell me a little about it."

"It really can be broken down into two elements. First, you can consider a domestic crime and second a gang-related crime.

"The first is the selling of babies and domestic workers. For example, maybe a couple wants to have children but cannot. Say they cannot pass a background check with an adoption agency, but they will gladly spend thirty to fifty thousand dollars to acquire a blonde-headed boy from Germany. No one knows where the dealer will fill the order, but you can bet it will not be legal. The couple pays the smuggler for the baby and takes delivery.

"Another example is filling domestic needs. Again, say an unscrupulous couple would like a live-in maid and babysitter. In Europe, it is called an Au Pair. They are almost impossible to find in the U.S., but for a substantial fee the dealer will locate a young, English-speaking female from a poor European or Baltic country. He promises the family that the girl will be placed with a wealthy U.S. family at no charge to her or her family. He may even offer the family some money. Supposedly, after three years she would have worked off her debt and be free to go, automatically becoming a citizen. Of course, this is not possible. Plus they tell the girl that if she does not continue to work until she is twenty-one, she will be deported or sent to jail. It is sort of soft slavery. Essentially, she ends up working for free for eight years and doesn't even have enough money to go home.

"Then on the dark side of human trafficking is the kidnapping of South American kids, smuggling them into the U.S. and selling them to the crime industry. The girls work as prostitutes and the boys become foot soldiers for the underworld gangland. The going price is about fifteen thousand dollars each. Most of them arrive in this country by boat. That would be where you guys could come in and help."

"Interesting, we will look into that with the Houston office."

As Commander Dickinson started walking to his door he said, "Enough of the heavy stuff, enjoy our city. Stay as long as you want. I think the Boss Man is just outside to show you our facilities."

As the lieutenant escorted them to the dormitory, Jack gave him one hundred dollars and the Boss Man said, "By the time you get ready to go, I'll have the tickets. The show opens in three hours and the Superdome is in walking distance. After the show, you might want to take a taxi to Bourbon Street. Oh, I also suggest you take a taxi back here any time after ten. Don't want to give the assholes a reason to stick a gun in your face. Just be aware and be safe."

The *Mad Max* premiere was a blast for the boys and mostly what they expected. About ten thousand crazies were inside the Superdome and almost all were wearing custom-made costumes. Most were not much more than a lot of tattoos, fake scars, and missing teeth but some were very creative and original. The most elaborate ones included a lot of leather, chains, animal skins, and some radical helmets or headdresses.

Jack said to Bear, "I'll bet the movie people are taking pictures for new ideas."

"Yeah, I am going to buy some of the posters to put on my wall."

Jack replied, "That will certainly impress the girls."

Bear ignored the comment and said, "You know, the thing I most noticed was the extreme makeup treatment of the eyes."

"I like it for us. It would change our looks a lot with not much effort."

After an hour or so the lights dimmed. It was showtime. The movie began with all the Superdome screens synced together. Most just stood on the field and watched the jumbo screen. On the way to Bourbon Street, they both agreed that *Thunderdome* was still the best. The crowds walking Bourbon Street were not much different than the ones they encountered at the *Mad Max* event. Maybe not as much makeup, but much rowdier.

The boys were told, "If you think this is wild, just come back during Mardi Gras."

A beer or two later and it was time to find a restaurant. Circling the block to Royal Street, they found several upscale establishments with white tablecloths. Unfortunately, the Boss Man did not inform them that most of these places had a dress code which did not include beach shorts and tee shirts. They finally settled for an Italian café that offered all-you-can-eat lasagna. After Bear finished, the restaurant most likely changed the menu to withdraw the all-you-can-eat posting.

It was not quite ten o'clock, so Jack and Bear began to walk Bourbon Street once again and continued to be amazed at the many bars. Bear stopped in front of one with a sign offering, *Have a Drink with the Most Beautiful Girls in New Orleans*. As they pushed open the saloon type doors, Bear already had his eyes on a tall blond seated by the bar.

He said, "Man she looks just like Kate," and started walking directly to her.

Jack was looking around and found that most of these ladies needed a shave. He said to Bear, "I'll bet ya a beer that you're ready to get out of here in five minutes."

"I'll take that bet. I think I am already in love."

Jack just stood back to watch as Bear walked to her, bent down, and whispered something in her ear. It is still not known what she said, but Bear stood straight up with his hands in the air, backed up, and shouted, "Jack, I owe you a beer."

Jack could not stop laughing as they left the bar. Bear said, "Jack, I swear to you that she sounded just like Chief Weatherford."

Still laughing, Jack pointed to the sign on the door which read, *Have a Drink with the Most Beautiful Queens of New Orleans*. "After you have had a few beers, you need to pay more attention to the advertising."

"Damn you Jack, don't tell anyone about this."

That did not stop the laughing.

"Well, let's go have a Hurricane. I heard it's a *must* when you visit New Orleans."

It was ten o'clock on the nose when they found *The Jazz Brothers*. The bouncer was at least as large as Bear, black, and looked a lot more dangerous. They gave him the tickets and mentioned that the Boss Man sent them.

"Well, I see you met my brother. Welcome, you guys part of the Coast Guard?"

"Yeah, sort of."

"Then follow me." He picked up an open table near the back and carried it next to the bandstand. "Excuse us, VIP's here," he said in a deep baritone voice.

No one complained and in fact they all shifted around to give some room and said, "No problem."

Jack looked at Bear, "The Boss Man rocks."

The music was good but the impromptu jazz was terrific.

Jack and Bear were back at the dorms by midnight and didn't wake up until o-six-hundred the next morning.

"Let's get moving Bear. We have a twelve-hour ride to Houston."

A quick goodbye and a thank you to the Boss Man and they were on their way.

Chapter 23

Castaway ducked into the jetty entrance at 5:00 PM (seventeen-hundred hours). They had about three hours of daylight left as they motored past Galveston and into the bay. It was astonishing to see a line of huge freighters and tankers entering the ship channel in route to their assigned terminals. Bear began to reminisce about his early life living in Galveston.

"In school, we were taught about Galveston's history. Back in the late 1800's when Texas was a new state and cotton was king, the industrial revolution was underway. European markets would eagerly buy all it could get. Galveston became a thriving shipping center, as it had a natural deep-water port and offered the cotton farmers much closer access to international shipping than the next nearest port in New Orleans.

"The problem was that it's an island. The cotton was shipped by rail to a gathering center in Houston and loaded on horse-drawn wagons. They then had to be carried seventy miles south and ferried across a bay before finally being loaded on the ships at Galveston Port."

Jack was mostly paying attention to his navigation, but was still listening, "That must have been a big effort."

Bear continued, "The decision to build a ship channel connecting directly to Houston made Galveston obsolete. It put overseas shipping and the railroads at one common trading center, offering easy loading and unloading."

"That and the hurricane that destroyed Galveston."

Jack's interest encouraged Bear to continue. "With commerce came the big banks. The refineries also began to pop up to take advantage of the international oil imports. Soon big oil began moving corporate offices to Houston. Now it's the second busiest port in the United States."

Jack replied, "It's amazing. If it weren't for shipping and air conditioning, Houston wouldn't even have twelve people living there and they would all be working for the post office. It would never have attracted the oil companies."

Bear noticed and pointed to the ships, "Do you know these giant boats are only moving at twelve knots in the channel, but because of their size and weight they require more than three miles to stop? And they cannot turn out of their locked paths. Even at that slow speed, the ships are moving about ten feet per second with no way to react to a sudden danger. The depth of the channel is forty feet deep but the bay is only about twenty. So it's like a train on tracks, they cannot independently change its course. The shipping lanes are barely wide enough to accommodate opposing traffic."

Jack added, "All the ships have radar, but the beam angle comes from the top which is sometimes more than ten stories high and mounted at the stern of the boat. The length and height of the front deck and its cargo causes close objects to be in a blind spot. Generally speaking, a small object less than three miles ahead is invisible,"

"How do they monitor that?"

"They don't. The only solution is that the big ships in the channel have the right-of-way. Everything else must just stay out of their way."

"I am surprised they don't have more collisions than they do."

Jack jumped back in, "Yeah, we studied that. Shipping is controlled and monitored by the Houston Port Authority. They are sort of like the airline's flight controllers. By the time the ship is within twenty miles of Galveston Island, they take control and monitor the vessel all the way to the terminals. A captain can lose his license if he does not comply with the Port Authority."

"Hey, Jack. I've seen pictures of big ships that have a giant torpedo-looking thing on the bow down low. What's that do?"

"Yeah. It is called a bulbous bow. It is located just below the waterline. The bulb modifies the water flow around the hull. It reduces drag and increases speed and fuel efficiency. It can stick out maybe thirty to forty feet and will cause a wave of water to rise in front of the ship maybe ten to fifteen feet."

The conversation went silent as Jack was concentrating on setting the navigation waypoints to guide them to the Coast Gard station safely.

Shortly after Bear asked, "Does Captain McCormick know our schedule?"

"Yeah, he said The Coast Guard would keep the lights on for us. Also, he wants to take us out to dinner for sort of a review and a celebration."

"Sounds okay, but I'm ready to get back to the Swordfish."

"What are you missing?" Jack asked.

"Marge's cooking."

"And what are you missing Jack?"

"Blimey."

The feel-good return to the Coast Guard station was interrupted by a distress call on the broadcast channel thirteen of the marine radio.

"Mayday, Mayday, is anyone near red buoy number eight? Need assistance immediately! Over."

Jack grabbed the radio mic and responded, "This is salvage ship *Castaway*. We are one mile from buoy number eight. How can we help? Over."

"This is shrimp boat *Stoker*. I am looking at a stalled fishing boat in the ship channel. An incoming cargo vessel is not a quarter mile away and charging fast. I cannot help. Over."

"We are on it. Over and Out."

Their adrenaline shot through the roof for both Jack and Bear. As Jack pushed the throttles to full speed, he shouted to Bear, "Go down and get the thirty foot and three-fourths inch dock line. Tie an end to the stern and coil the rest. Get ready to jump in the boat."

Jack called out on the radio, "Captain of the container ship, cut your props. Over."

"Already did that. Over."

"Wish me luck."

Jack thought, *If the shrimper is correct, we will get there at the exact same time the freighter does. Hope he's wrong.*

The nearest freighter to red buoy number eight was just about a half mile ahead. *Castaway* closed the distance in only thirty seconds. They could now see the small fishing craft with a man and a woman screaming and waving their arms. The freighter was five stories high, not one hundred and fifty feet away and closing in at ten feet per second. A collision was less than fifteen seconds away.

Jack used the loudspeaker, "Stay in the boat."

He shouted to Bear, "Let me get next to the boat, then jump. Hold on for your life, the line will jerk when I start pulling." Jack quickly positioned *Castaway* for a very close pass.

Bear jumped into the boat with a flop, landing in the open front bow. He wrapped the line around his waist and laid down on the floor with his feet in front of him with each foot on the fiberglass bow. To minimize the jerk, Jack slightly accelerated to uncoil the line. The freighter was now within thirty feet and the bulbous bow actually passed below the fishing boat causing it to rise rapidly. Castaway began to pull. When Jack saw the line become taut, he pushed the throttles to one-third, causing the light fishing boat to rocket forward while the wave was lifting it upward. It miraculously stayed upright and was safely skating outside the channel. Jack continued for another three hundred yards before stopping.

The shrimp boat radioed, "They did it! Great job *Castaway*."

The freighter captain responded, "Thank you, I owe you a big one *Castaway*."

Most every boat in Galveston Bay was listening to the rescue effort and as the shrimp boat announced the success each sounded their horns, causing quite a celebration.

Jack brought the fishing boat alongside *Castaway* while Bear secured the lines and helped the couple onto the stern deck. Jack quickly handed down the sleeping bags. The girl was in shock and the guy was as white as a ghost. Jack used the secure radio to call the Coast Guard.

Captain McCormick answered with, "Yes, I heard everything on the radio. Bring them in, I have already called an ambulance."

Jack responded with the condition of the couple and estimated they could be docked in less than thirty minutes. Unbeknownst to Jack, McCormick had also called the local T.V. station to see if they wanted to cover the rescue. Of course they were more than interested and sent their best news crew for the interview.

KTRN Eyewitness News arrived at the Coast Guard station as the ambulance was packing up. The couple was now sitting and didn't require more immediate medical assistance. However, the EMS informed them that they must go to the hospital for a trauma check. The news team quickly set up their gear and then turned to the reporter with a thumbs-up.

A gorgeous brunette looked into the camera and said, "We are standing on the docks of the Galveston Bay Coast Guard station, where a dangerous and daring rescue was successful in saving the lives of this young couple. It seems that an enjoyable afternoon fishing trip turned disastrous when their engine developed trouble and left them drifting. Without an anchor, the wind pushed them into the ship channel in front of an incoming freighter. Avoiding the deadly tragedy were two courageous men who came to the rescue with only seconds to spare." She then turned her attention to the young man and asked, "Oh my God, what a story. What is your name?"

"Jerry and I am still a little shaken up."

"Well, I can imagine. Are you sure that you don't need medical attention?"

"Not right now. I am just thankful that we are here talking to you."

"Is your girlfriend alright?"

"She is not my girlfriend. She is my sister Vicky, but she just wants to go home."

"May I ask her a question?"

"Sure."

"Miss, are you okay?"

She was wet and cold with a blanket around her shoulders. She looked like she just stepped out of a horror movie as she stood and said, "I'm so grateful we are alive." She then put her arm around her brother, looked straight into the camera, laughed and said, "I will never go fishing with him again." She pointed, "We owe our lives to these two brave men. I cannot believe they were able to make the rescue."

Jack and Bear came walking over and hugged them both without saying a word. The medics interrupted and insisted they must get them to the hospital now and escorted the couple to the ambulance. The TV crew immediately pivoted to Jack and Bear.

"You guys are heroes. Please tell us your names."

"My name is Jack Mahan and this is my partner, Bear DeMarco."

"You risk your lives to make that rescue. Why did you do it?"

Jack answered, "If we didn't do it, who would?"

"But you could have died."

Bear was shaking his head, "Yes, we missed it by a whole two seconds. Just as Jack jerked the line to pull us away, I looked up and saw a five-story giant coming at us at ten feet a second. I knew I was dead."

Jack added, "Yeah, we don't want to do that again."

"Here we are standing on these docks. Are you part of the Coast Guard?"

"No, we are just a small salvage ship," and pointed to the sign on the side of *Castaway*'s tower that said *Sanford Salvage and Water Repairs*.

Captain McCormick moved in to ask the TV crew to wrap-up as he needed to ask the young men some questions.

"Okay, we will keep up with this story as it develops. I am Lesley Townsend, KTRN Eyewitness News.

The news crew started to pack their equipment, as Jack, Bear and Captain McCormick began to walk back to the station.

"You guys have had enough today, let's just go have a few beers. I found a new seafood place called Cap'n Benny's. Cold beer and great food."

"Sounds great, but not until I take a cold shower. I still need to get my heart rate down."

Bear said, "Is that because of the rescue or the cute T.V. girl?"

Jack smiled, reached into his pocket, and pulled out a business card. It read *Lesley Townsend, KTRN Eyewitness News* and a handwritten note that said "call me" and her phone number. The next day started at daybreak with Captain McCormick bringing a bag full of breakfast from McDonald's.

"Let's get started, we have a lot to do. For your information, the fishing boat was just out of gas. However, the gauge indicated half full, obviously broken. Another case of a citizen boater not checking all systems before motoring off to dangerous waters."

Sarcastically Jack said, "Thank you for that, I get your warning."

"Can you guys be ready to roll for us in a week or two?"

"No way," Jack said, "We need time to finish the inside of the boat and begin to load up the tools needed to do both salvage and spook work."

"What do you need?"

"Below deck, we need to build a small crane to lift equipment in and out of the hull. Then a tool room area with an assortment of tools we may need and an inflatable boat with a fifty-horse outboard."

"Okay, that doesn't sound like it will take very long. What else?"

"We are going simple with the furnishings but we are tired of camping out onboard. However, we are not going to skimp on the infrastructure just a big air conditioning system, plumbing, and electrical.

"I understand. How about I give you ninety days?"

Jack looked over at Bear for an answer. Bear said, "Depends on if we can get the equipment shipped in on time. We are working at the end of the world down there."

"Okay, we shoot for ninety days and look at it then."

"You got a deal," they both said.

"Your shipment of ammunition arrived last week. We will help you store it in the locked storage room in the hull of the boat. I am glad we put that in the center of the ship. The total weight is more than two thousand pounds. If you run low, we will ship you more."

Jack joked, "Crap, that's enough to start a war."

"You will be surprised how quickly you use it with the machine guns."

"Can we use it for target practice?"

"Sure, how else are you going to become an expert? By the way, when we finish loading the ammo, pull around to our pumps and we will top your tank off."

Castaway and the boys were ready to make the final leg of their long trip that started from the Curtis Bay shipyards in Maryland. With good weather, the journey to the Swordfish would likely take twenty hours at a comfortable cruising speed of thirty knots. It should put them home by mid-morning. Jack called the marina and talked to Marge. She was excited and told him that the slip has been ready for some time. She said that Bud had built a dock away from the public boats to give some privacy.

"Call me when you are a few miles out. We have a surprise for you."

Chapter 24

It was a long, yet fulfilling journey from the shipyard in Maryland to South Texas and the boys were anxious to get home. After leaving the Galveston jetties, they turned south straight to the Swordfish. The overnight trip was uneventful except for the abundance of fish, especially during the early hours of the next morning. Just after sunup, they picked up an escort of dolphins which played Follow the Leader with *Castaway* for at least an hour. Littering the route were dozens of offshore oil structures. An unusually large one was directly in their path. Jack slowed to inspect the structure and the dolphin game quickly stopped. They began to spread out as if spooked.

Bear pointed to several shark fins coming in fast from the structure. Apparently, they were ready for breakfast. As quickly as the sharks arrived, the dolphins disappeared, leaving the sharks circling the boat.

Bear counted at least ten and said, "That looks nasty."

"Yeah, I would not like to be in the water just now."

"We have a lot of food in the ice chest that we need to dump. Let's see what they'll do if I throw it out."

Jack laughed and said, "Don't slip and fall overboard."

They had some snacks and lunch meat but nothing large enough to make a meal for a hungry shark. However, it did cause some excitement as the sharks went into a feeding frenzy. They came up to the stern of *Castaway* and even tried to take a bite of the steel rudder, causing the wheel in the bridge to jerk. As the sharks gave up and began to leave, Jack noticed a school of king mackerel in the shade of the platform. The sharks also became aware of them and the race was on.

Jack idled down to watch as the sharks became pack hunters. They organized and surrounded the mackerel. Once the circle was complete, the killing began. For the next few minutes, the waters were thrashing and seemed to boil as the sea turned blood red. Just as quickly, the water smoothed, the sharks left, and the only hints of carnage were a few pieces of scales and intestines. Jack quietly pushed the throttles forward to level off at their cruising speed of thirty knots.

Bear, still with his eyes wide open, said, "Man, I have never seen anything like that."

Jack replied, "Ya know, I was thinking about taking a quick swim to freshen up for our return, but you couldn't pay me enough money to do it now.

"I agree, we will just come home stinky."

"That is why we need full plumbing, including hot water, in this boat."

"It's on the list."

When they passed the next platform, they noticed a flash coming from under the structure. Continuing to watch, the boys saw a giant grey form. It was hard to identify in the deep blue water. *Castaway* was not more than two hundred feet from the structure when the monster became visible. The hammerhead shark's fin surfaced as it swam up to investigate the invaders.

"Look at the size of that thing," yelled Bear. It was huge, about half as long as *Castaway* which made it almost twenty-five to thirty feet long. "I see how it gets its name, the head is the shape of a sledgehammer with each side extending past its body by maybe two feet. That big boy looks dangerous."

The shark eventually lost interest and returned to the shadows of the platform. Out of curiosity, they slowed down to take a look each time they passed near other structures. In almost every case the cover provided by the pilings and the shadow of the platform itself attracted fish of all types, but sharks were harder to spot. Most of the structures were set on the ocean floor in over ninety feet of water, making it impossible to see the bottom. However, they frequently noticed large, dark movements which seemed to circle the pilings.

With less than an hour to go, Jack called the Swordfish on the marine satellite phone. Marge answered with her cheerful voice, and when she realized it was Jack, she screamed, "Oh my God, I was hoping it was you!"

"Hi Marge, we will be there at about thirteen hundred hours."

She interrupted, "What did you say?"

"Oh, I forgot. That is military time for 1:00 o'clock."

"Whatever, I don't understand that stuff, but I'm so happy. We thought it was about time for you guys to show up."

"Where do you want us to park the boat?"

"Just come into the visitor area, near the fuel pumps. We'll be waiting for ya."

Marge and Bud were standing on the dock, along with several other onlookers. Blimey was sitting attentively at the feet of Marge. A deeply-tanned and lanky individual was standing in the shadows behind the crowd. He was wearing a large-brimmed Panama hat with long white hair covering his ears and sporting a full white beard. He seemed to be smiling as he watched *Castaway* back into the visitor slip.

Who is that guy? thought Jack.

Positioned on the stern deck, Bear passed the docking lines to Bud and soon had the boat secured. Jack shut down the engines. Amid whistles, shouting, and clapping, Jack rushed down to embrace Marge and Blimey. The onlookers were waiting to shake hands with the boys, but Jack's attention was on the stranger. He had a familiar look.

As the crowd began to thin, Bud walked over and put his hand on Jack's shoulder and said as he gestured to the stranger, "Let me introduce my long-lost brother, but you may remember him as your father."

The smile on Jack's face changed to a curious frown and stared at the stranger for a few moments. When the concept sank in, he broke into a jog to face the man, "Is it really you?"

Eddie reached and put both arms around Jack and said, "Yes and man have I missed you."

The tears and shouts of joy remained the mood most of the afternoon. Bear shuffled up to Eddie and stuck out his massive hand. "My name is Bear, I've heard a lot about you. It's an honor to meet you."

Eddie responded, "Likewise, welcome to the family."

Bud broke in, "You can leave the boat here for tonight. We'll take care of it tomorrow."

The five of them plus Blimey moved to the café as Marge teased, "Anyone want a hamburger?"

The café was empty but the noise from the table sounded like a neighborhood pub on a Saturday night. Marge served the group cold beer. Each tried to talk at once, but when the food arrived, all conversation stopped. Blimey even had his sample of grilled meat. Bear said, "This is about the best hamburger I've ever had."

Bud grabbed everyone's attention and said, "Eddie has been here for a few weeks, and I have thoroughly informed him of the contract agreement with the Coast Guard.

Eddie jumped in, "Sounds like a sweet deal, I am very proud of you guys. Congrats! I want to know all about it later when we can get into the details. But for me, I'll be working here for a while. Our group is now back in the states for as long as it takes to replenish our piggy bank. We had some storm damage plus we need new sails. The sailboat is currently sitting at a marina in Australia. Hopefully, we will be able to continue our venture in maybe six months.

Bud added, "Eddie now has his captain's license and he has been delivering boats whenever and wherever he can. Of course, he is working around here and hiring out with the fishing fleet."

Jack questioned, "Hope you are staying with Bear and me at the beach house."

Bud interrupted, "Before we do that, let me tell you of some changes I have made. We have built you a private slip on the back side of the marina. It also has a sizeable closed-in work shed attached. It is large enough to store the parts and tools needed to finish out the boat. It is air-conditioned and has a small bedroom. It will be Bear's quarters, I think he needs his privacy. He can use the marina's showers and bathrooms. It frees up the beach house to accommodate Jack and his father."

Bear, Jack and Eddie all responded in sync with, "perfect".

The rest of the evening was spent listening to Eddie tell of his adventures island-hopping in the South Pacific.

The next morning, Bud and Eddie wanted to see the camo conversion but Jack explained the security reasons why he couldn't do it while docked.

Bear said, "Hey, we have to move it anyway, let's take it out of the marina and we can even demo the machine guns?"

Being a gun guy, Bud got excited. "Great idea. I even know where we can find a half-sunken shrimp boat we can use for target practice."

All four guys and Blimey climbed on board and were out to open water within thirty minutes. Bear explained what they saw as he operated the camo conversion controls. He took Bud and Eddie down to the deck to get one of the fifty-caliber machine guns ready.

Jack positioned the *Castaway* to within fifty yards of the shipwreck and in ten feet of water. "I'll keep her right here, fire at will."

Bear stepped through the details of using the machine gun, gave them ear protectors, and ask them to stand back as he aimed. The sound was deafening as ten rounds exploded into the target in less than two seconds. They were amazed at the vast, gaping holes along the side of the shrimper.

"Here, Bud. You try it."

Bud took a wide stance and aimed at the control tower. After a ten second burst, he began to shout, "Holy smoke that was fun!"

The bridge was now laying on its side and hanging on by the wiring and cables. Eddie took his turn with an equal response. After a couple more practice shoots, Jack hit the camo control buttons and they watched the boat revert back to a harmless salvage vessel.

On the way back, they were all up on the bridge when Jack slammed the throttles to full speed. The massive engines came alive like thoroughbred racehorses coming out of the starter's gate. Not knowing what to expect, the g-force slammed Bud and Eddie to the rear wall and sent them scrambling for something to grab. Within ten seconds, the boat was passing through forty knots.

"Unbelievable!" shouted Eddie.

They eased into the Swordfish and skillfully backed into *Castaway*'s new home.

"Okay, what's next?" asked Bud.

"The Coast Guard has given us ninety days to finish out the insides. We most likely can't do it all, but we can make it usable by then. This work shed is going to help. We can start ordering the parts and store them in the shed until we need them."

Continuing to question, Bud asked, "Well, what ya have in mind?"

"We are going simple with the furnishings, but we are tired of using a port-a-potty. However, we are not going to skimp on the infrastructure and get a big air conditioning system, plumbing, and electrical.

"Okay, I understand that."

"We are talking refrigeration big enough to cool the entire tower and the forward storage area below deck. Stub it in now and finish it out later."

"Okay, that doesn't sound like it will take very long. What else?"

"Well, on the way down here, Bear and I have made a pretty good list. We want to do the below deck work with equipment that will serve our needs now and in the future. As we said, we are not concerned with the furnishings in the tower. We just need it to be functional. We can make it nice later on."

"Keep going."

"The big jobs are in the engine room. We need a diesel powered 115-volt generator with enough power to run the air conditioning, various lighting needs, the crane winch, and other salvage work needs. The existing hydraulic system needs to be modified and expanded to run hydraulic lines to the front for future salvage needs.

"The freshwater system is pretty straightforward in comparison. Some of the desalination water makers come as completed bolt-in kits. We need to convert sea water to drinkable water at maybe twenty-five to fifty gallons per hour and store at least two hundred gallons. Of course, we need a water heater for the kitchen and showers.

"We must have proper plumbing. It should also be pretty easy to install by following the standard marine procedures of holding tanks, pumps, grinders, and bypass valves. The electrical system should include a switch-over panel to support shore power, generator power, or the 12-volt boat power. We must support floodlights on the front and rear decks and a large freezer locker located somewhere below deck and accessible."

Bud sat back in his chair, "That is quite a list, but we still have quite a lot of money in the bank and most of this is readily available. Anymore big stuff?"

"Yes, but I think it could be simple. Below the forward deck, we need to design a small folding crane to lift equipment in and out of the hull. It must be designed to store below deck. Then a tool room area with an assortment of tools we may need and an inflatable boat with a fifty-horse outboard."

"That doesn't seem to be difficult. Just some design work and welding," said Eddie.

Bear spoke up, "Once we have all of this done, we can do a quick but temporary finish out of the kitchen, bathroom, and bedrooms."

Bud was intently listening and said, "I have a suggestion for the inside finish out. I still have the old travel trailer that Marge and I lived in while we were building the house. You can have it. Just scavenge all the built-ins and reinstall in the tower. Simple. Quick. Done!"

"Uncle Bud, you are a genius."

Eddie had been taking this all in and blurted out an offer, "You guys pay me the same as I would make as a deckhand and I will have the trailer conversion done in a month. I am good at woodworking and remodeling."

Jack pointed to his dad and said, "And you too are a genius."

At the two-month point, Captain McCormick arrived at the Swordfish for a situational checkup. The finish-out was complete and the boys were working on the mechanics of the foldable crane. They assured the Captain that within a week the job would be done.

"Good, because we may have an opportunity to put some serious hurt on one of the major drug suppliers in Texas. Right now we have the leader of the largest drug gang in Texas cooling his heels in the county jail, awaiting trial. If we can bust this one, narcotics will become a rare commodity in North Texas for some time. However, it's not just him we want. I think we can also bust the major cartel distributor."

"How would we be involved?"

"We believe the Columbian Cartel ships its narcotics, both cocaine and heroin, by boat. It always stays out in international waters. A US-flagged boat, disguised as a fishing vessel, will meet the supply boat to transfer money for drugs. Your job would be to track the fishing boat back inside the twelve-mile limit and hand them over to us."

"How are we to know which boat to track?"

"This is where it gets complicated. With the leader in jail, the DEA and the Dallas drug unit believe they can infiltrate the gang to get the operational information. We are currently looking for an undercover agent who can pull it off. We have some cops that are willing, but we need a new face. We are looking for someone with old Mafia ties, maybe from Chicago. You know, someone that is hard to trace down and hard to check out.

"We will keep you posted, but be ready to go on short notice."

The finishing touches were complete and the overnight shakedown cruise proved all systems were operating flawlessly.

As *Castaway* was entering the Swordfish harbor, Bear said, "Jack, I've been thinking about taking some time off."

"What do you mean?"

"We worked hard last year, don't you think?"

"Sure. We've accomplished a lot in that year."

"Yeah, I would like some downtime."

Jack smiled and looked over at Bear, "You've been thinking about Kate again, haven't you?"

"Yeah, we talk almost every week and she wants me to fly in for a visit."

"Well, we are ahead of schedule, and I think we deserve it."

"What do you mean 'we'?"

Jack reached into his back pocket, brought out his wallet, and found the business card that read, "Lesley Townsend, KTRN Eyewitness News," with a handwritten note to call her at her home phone number.

"Yeah Bear, I think we could both use some R&R."

Part Seven

Cujo – The Cocaine King

Chapter 25

In the months before the boys returned to the Swordfish, Rex Sampson was making the most of his firm's yacht, *Judgement*. His partners were always joking about using the boat enough to justify the IRS deduction. In the summer season, they were entertaining clients and other influential business associates on an average of three to four times per month. The guests seemed to be thrilled to experience big time sport-fishing. Both the "Sports" pages and the "Society" section of the *Dallas Morning News* regularly featured articles which included pictures. It was working just as the partners had hoped.

Being a law firm and keenly conscious of liability risks, they agreed to hire a professional captain and deckhands for these occasions. When Rex consulted Bud to help find a crew, naturally Eddie was recommended. He had his commercial captain's license, experience, was responsible, and even had years of involvement in deep-sea fishing. Rex made a conditional offer contingent on a successful trial run.

Eddie put out flyers in the neighboring villages and found some excellent experienced deckhands who wanted the work. None could speak English, but it was of no concern to Eddie as he spoke fluent Spanish. Eddie settled on Julio and his brother Marco and offered them a total of two hundred and fifty dollars per day.

During the trial, they caught and released a small sailfish and had several other excellent strikes. Returning to the marina, Eddie backed into the slip and secured the yacht while Julio and Marco cleaned the boat until it was spotless.

Rex and Eddie were both satisfied and before Rex returned to Dallas, they negotiated a fee of one thousand dollars per day which included bait, deckhand duties, and boat detailing after each trip, but offered no guarantees of catching fish. Guests could of, course, tip the deckhands if they felt inclined to do so.

As the summer progressed, Rex and Eddie's friendship grew and they became almost as close as brothers. Frequently, in the evenings and after the clients were gone, they would sit in the luxurious open mezzanine and drink a few cold beers with Eddie who told of his experiences island-hopping in the South Pacific.

Fishing season was ending as the abundance of billfish had moved south for the winter. It was the time of the year for the law partners to begin to think about other options for family enjoyment. *Judgment* was taking a back seat in choosing between the hunting lodge in Montana, the gentle breezes of Maui, or the ski slopes of Vail.

It was in fact, the last day of September and Rex and Eddie were having dinner at the Swordfish. With maybe a beer or two too many, Rex began to talk about himself.

"You know Eddie, we are about the same age."

"Yeah, what about it."

"Well, sometimes I feel guilty. Just look at us. You are at ease with yourself, living a simple yet thrilling life and have few worries that I can see."

Eddie put down his beer and said, "Do you want to trade?"

Rex laughed, "No, that's not what I am trying to say. You seem happy with yourself, plus the father of a superior son with a bright future ahead of him. Hell, if he or Bear was an attorney, I would hire them both."

"Thank you for your comments. We have been very fortunate."

Rex thought a moment and said, "What do you mean by the term 'we'? Do you still believe that your wife influences Jack after all these years?"

"I am sure she does somewhat, but I was referring to our family here."

Rex looked at Eddie with tears in his eyes and said, "I still cannot get over my children. Their death was so senseless and unnecessary. That's what

I meant by guilt. I sometimes believe I took my career more seriously than my fatherhood."

Looking to Eddie for help, he said, "Well, aren't you going to agree? Most people do."

Eddie became very serious, "Don't make me the example of a good father. I never even provided a proper home or embraced a family environment. Hell Rex, I married a hippie and we did not have a real home until Jack was ten. We lived the life of gypsies, spending six months in the mountains and six months here. During that time I would be absent for weeks, leaving Jack with a babysitter while I traveled off to chase some new exciting challenge or adventure. Yeah, the time we spent was good, but if you want to find a better example of parenting look at my brother."

"Bud?"

"Yeah and Marge."

Rex countered, "Bud was not grounded either. How could a professional gambler be a good influence?"

"If you are looking for answers just blame genetics. I have seen it a thousand times at Vail. Most of the kids are spoiled brats that have never heard the word 'no'. As I saw them grow up, they were essentially worthless. Then the next kid came along and was keenly attentive, worked hard, and grew up successful, both from the same wealthy and loving parents. If you think I did a good job as a dad, thank you, but I had very little to do with it. I do agree about one thing, Jack has it and so does Bear. They are both solid and know the difference between right and wrong. Two different backgrounds, so what else can it be but the luck of the draw?"

"I appreciate that, but it still eats at my guts. I should have seen the narcotic thing."

Just before calling it an evening, Marge busted in and said, "You guys need to stay put a little longer. We have a meeting. Bud and the boys are on the way."

After they all clambered in and found a seat around the table, Bud announced, "Captain McCormick wants us to fly to Houston tomorrow. It seems an opportunity now exists for a huge bust. Maybe large enough to break the back of the drug industry for a while in most of Texas. We must move fast.

He'll send the Learjet down to pick us up in the morning. Rex, he would like you to attend."

"Okay."

"You should spend the night on your boat."

Rex said, "That's fine. I'm in no condition to drive anyway."

"We should be back by late afternoon."

Eddie said, "Sounds like you guys may be getting busy." Looking over at Rex, he added, "I have some straightening up to do on *Judgement* before putting her up for the season. It'll be bright and shiny when you return with no signs of fishing poles or ice chests."

Chapter 26

The conference room chatter stopped as Captain McCormick entered and closed the door behind him. "You all appear to be in a good mood after the speedy ride to Houston. Welcome and I am pleased to see Mr. Sampson could join us. Are you guys and your ship ready for action?"

Jack took the lead and replied, "Yes sir, the boat is ready for most anything. Bear and I are looking forward to testing our skills."

"Great, I am excited to launch our first mission, *Operation Yellow Jacket*. You may find some humor with the name, as we will be setting up a sting tactic to capture the drug cartel as they attempt to smuggle narcotics into Texas."

Bud asked, "What do you have in mind?"

"Without getting into the details just yet, let me first give you an overview. Essentially, the targeted gang controls the distribution and sale of cocaine and heroin to the entire Dallas/Fort Worth Metroplex."

Bear raised his hand and asked, "Do you know the name of the group?"

"Not exactly, they use a lot of names as it is regional in structure. Think of it as various retail shoe outlets all over Texas. Each operate with different store names, yet all are selling the same product. The organization that we are targeting is the distributor to the neighborhood gangs. These guys just want to sell narcotics."

"Okay, then how do we get involved? "

"Most of the source, or manufacturing of the drugs and its packaging, is done in Central America. The various governments down there are paid off by the cartels and therefore are mostly left alone. The most significant problem for them is exporting the drugs to their distribution partners. Small shipments are routinely smuggled through Mexico and into Texas. However, they are prone to police interdiction. Therefore most of the high-value mass deliveries are by sea. They know that we, the Coast Guard, are not authorized to patrol in international waters, so they have designed a system to offer maximum protection. The master supply ship will stay outside this limit and let the distributor, typically disguised as a fishing boat, come out to them to pick up their inventory. It will be here where we can intercept the shipment between the supply boat and the Texas coast."

"That sounds easy enough, but how will we know which fishing boat to follow, we can't watch the entire Texas gulf coast."

"This is where the sting occurs. We plan to infiltrate the organization with an undercover agent. He should be able to get the information such as where the boat is based and the location and timing of the delivery."

"Now that sounds a little more difficult."

Captain McCormick took a drink of water and continued, "Exactly, but here is where we may have a break which will make the sting much more accessible and less dangerous. Circumstances have occurred which demand that we move within the next few weeks. Rex, this is where you may be needed to arrange some favors with the press and police force.

"Again, we haven't flushed out the plan, but the head or boss of the North Texas operation is now in jail in Dallas County awaiting trial for trafficking narcotics. It was a weak arrest as the cops did not get a proper search warrant after they stopped him for a traffic violation. He may walk soon, as his attorney is working for his release now. His name is Deuce Rodriquez. I suppose the name 'Deuce' represents the two cities. The FBI believes he has killed more than five men and should be considered an extremely dangerous character. At least eight captains run the street gangs. They control the narcotics trade throughout the Metroplex. With Rodriquez out of the picture, the FBI and the DEA are of the opinion that we can initiate a coup and insert a new leader, essentially taking over the smuggling operations."

"That sounds bloody."

"Not if the new leader brings in the force of the mafia or at least they believe the mafia is behind the coup. These guys only understand force."

Bud was thinking about it and said, "Do you have this super-spy mafia insurgent identified yet."

"No, it is dangerous and it has to be a perfect fit. If suspected of being a plant, the gang will instantly kill the agent. If we can't find one, we will pass the project. The FBI has a couple of prospects from Chicago but don't want to pull them out of their current assignments. We are still looking."

Jack asked, "What are the requirements?"

"He must be fluent in Spanish, be between thirty to forty-five years old, in shape, a quick thinker, good communicator, and a cool operator. Most of all, they will not panic and can be trusted."

"I think you just described my father."

Bud shouted out, "My God, you are right."

Rex slowly stood up and said, "It hurts me to say this as I may lose my yacht captain, but I can certainly recommend Eddie. In fact, I insist."

Bud held both hands up with his palms out and said, "Wait! We have to discuss this with Eddie. He must know what he is getting into and the dangers at hand. Can we call you tomorrow?"

Back at the Swordfish, the guys spent two hours discussing the facts presented by Captain McCormick. Eddie quietly sat at the table, took it all in, and stated, "You know I've been getting a little restless and need some new excitement. Answer me just one question. What's in it for me?"

Jack, Bud, and Bear agreed to split any reward money just like the old pirates did. Divide into seven equal parts. Three parts would go to the boat and one part to each person.

Eddie had a quick response, "Deal. Plus they must pay any out of pocket expenses and when this is over they fly me back to Australia first class."

A call to Captain McCormick informed of the conditions Eddie needed. They struck an agreement and a new chapter in Eddie's life as an undercover agent had begun.

The Captain added, "Give me a day to make the arrangements and I will have the Learjet down to pick him up. He needs to bring as little as possible as he will begin the transformation to a new temporary identity. He will be picked up by an FBI agent and taken to the Dallas field office. Tell him to expect a two-week stay to train. It will take them that long to arrange the supporting cast and build the structure of the story. He will have a secure phone and can talk to you guys most any time. It the meantime, prepare your ship for battle. Oh, I forgot, tell Eddie that he may terminate the operation at any time, for any reason."

Chapter 27

A tall, strikingly beautiful Latina wearing a black short skirt, white silk blouse, and spike heels was waiting in the lounge area of the busy Private Aviation Terminal at Love Field. As Eddie entered the terminal, he was to meet an FBI agent and his expectations did not include the one that fit her description. He continued to steal glances at the exotic woman while scanning the crowd to identify a tough looking guy with short hair and a badge.

When the area began to clear, she walked up and asked, "Eddie Mahan?"

Eddie tried not to stare when he answered with a sheepish, "Yes."

With a professional smile, she stuck out her hand, "Hello, my name is Zoe Castillo with the FBI. Welcome to Dallas."

Eddie thought as he continued to gawk, *I think I'm going to like this assignment.*

Zoe said, "I have been given the responsibility to guide you through the training. I am a disguise artist, but I will also shape your attitude to match the profile we need. They tell me you speak Spanish. It is a must for this character. To start, you and I will only speak the Latin language for a while. Are you okay with that?"

Eddie responds in Spanish, "[Yes] Sí."

Zoe asked, "[Do you have any luggage?] ¿Tienes equipaje?"

"[Just this carry on.] Solo esto continua."

Zoe then motioned with her arm, "[The car is waiting outside.] El auto está esperando afuera."

"[Where are we going?]"

"[To the FBI field office in downtown Dallas.]"

After getting in the car, Zoe said, "Okay, I am satisfied with your language skills. Now down to business. You will be a Puerto Rican who earned a name for yourself with the local mafia there. You were picked up by the Cosa Nostra and moved to Philadelphia. After a few years, you became part of The Family. You cannot get any better than that. More on the mob later. Now we must give you a name. I have come up with Carlos Jekel. Are you familiar with the horror characters in Doctor Jekyll and Mr. Hyde? You will become Doctor Jekel for your enemies and just Doc for your friends. Any objections?"

"Doc Jekel, I like it. Might get some respect."

The driver dropped them off at a non-descript, twenty-story bank building in the financial district. Zoe explained that the FBI prefers to keep a somewhat low profile and not attract attention.

Eddie thought, *Yeah and they think you don't attract attention.*

She continued, "We occupy the entire tenth and eleventh floors."

After a few introductions to the agents covering the case, she escorted Eddie to her laboratory. She explained, "Here we will give you a new look to go along with your new name. Make yourself comfortable in this barber chair while I bring a few pictures. By the way, for the next few weeks, you will only answer to the names Carlos, Carlos Jekel, Doctor Jekel, or Doc. Got it?" After looking at many pictures of real Mafia characters, she said, "Considering your new Spanish heritage in Puerto Rico, I think we should have the look of a charismatic Latino 'man-about-town'. However, if crossed, he would quickly kill."

"Let's go for it."

"First, we need to get rid of the grey hair, but I can work with the length. You will have a mustache but it will be fake because facial hair grows very fast. Plus you might need to change identity quickly and removing the mustache might give you a little time. Just relax and let me do my job."

Within two hours, the transformation was complete. The hair was black mixed with a very dark brown highlight which was trimmed and groomed by combing it straight back and into a small ponytail or sort of a bun. The beard was gone and in its place was a medium thick mustache with its ends turning down and growing past his mouth line. Some would call it a Fu Manchu, or a Joe Namath look.

When Eddie stared into the mirror, he asked in Spanish, "[How do I look?] ¿Cómo se ve esto?"

Zoe stepped back and said, "[Magnificent, you are very sexy.] Magnífico, eres muy sexy."

Eddie continued to admire his new image, "Yeah, I think I may keep this look."

"Let's take a break Carlos. This afternoon we'll go buy your new clothes."

For Eddie, shopping was not one of his favorite things to do, but shopping with Zoe was delightful. Spending the afternoon in Dallas upscale men's stores resulted in just what she wanted. First was a two thousand dollar, dark grey suit, a pair of black alligator dress shoes with pointed toes for another thousand dollars, two black silk dress shirts, and two black pullover, turtleneck golf shirts.

She explained, "The Cosa Nostra, especially in the Northeast, love expensive clothes but never wear a tie. With what we picked out, the gang will immediately identify you as a member of the mob. Starting tomorrow, you will also need to learn how to act like it."

Back at the Swordfish Marina, Jack, Bear, and Bud were busy making last minute preparations. The boat was ready but they needed to complete their disguise outfits. They brought all the items they collected along the way and stacked the costumes in a pile at the back of the cafe. Looking at the pile of junk was when they realized that having an idea and making it work was a step that was beyond them.

Marge walked in with Blimey and asked, "What are you guys up to now?"

Bud said, "I think we are over our heads. Maybe you can help?

After listening to the problem, she smiled and said, "I once did some work for the high school drama department. Let me see what you have and your ideas. I will need to get some paint and theatrical makeup. I should have this done in a week. Go do something else, I am in charge of this."

Chapter 28

The Special Delivery package arrived midmorning, causing quite a stir at the Swordfish. Noticing it was from the Coast Guard, Marge immediately called another meeting. Ten minutes later, she carefully read the notice to Bud and the boys:

> *To: Sanford Salvage and Water Repairs*
> *From: Captain Brad McCormick, Managing Director*
> *Marine Safety and Security Team*
> *Secret Document: Do not discuss the contents with anyone outside the MSST.*
>
> *Operation Yellow Jacket is now activated and will meet at the headquarters in Houston to begin tactical planning.*
>
> *We will need you to relocate your vessel from the Swordfish to the Houston Coast Guard facility. Be moored at our docks by 0800 hours on Wednesday. Plan on staying there for at least two weeks.*
>
> *I know this will sound strange but bring your dog, Blimey. We need to record the narcotics transactions on the boats. They will search Eddie for a wire and to get around that we have an idea of fitting a recorder on Blimey that would look like a typical dog tag.*

We need to do some testing to see if it will work and if Blimey will act as usual before we commit to the plan.

Attending this meeting will be the FBI, DEA, Eddie, his handler, and Rex Sampson.

Situations are present that demand quick actions. It is what we hoped for, so we need to get to work.

Good luck and see you in two days.

Jack asked, "Marge, have you finished the costumes?"

"Yes, but we need to try them on to make sure they fit."

Bear added, "Will do. Looks like this is it, I think we are ready."

Bud reached down to pat Blimey on the head and said, "Hey, you're even going to get into the action. Quite a family we have here!"

Jack said, "Okay you guys, get packed. We need to leave in an hour."

At Wednesday's sunrise, Bud and the boys were having breakfast at the Coast Guard's cafeteria when Captain McCormick plopped down beside them and said, "Are you ready to kick some ass?"

The group laughed and gave high-fives to all and said, "Good morning Captain, sit down and have a cup of coffee with us."

"I will take one to go. I need to get the conference room ready for the presentation. Relax, enjoy the morning, and I'll see you guys at 0900 hours. Big day!"

Blimey barked hello.

The rest of the team arrived in bulk as an Air Force shuttle bus delivered them from Ellington Air Field. After a noisy hello, they all settled into the chairs around the conference table. Captain McCormick's introductions included the regional head of DEA, the FBI's Dallas Field Director, Howard Suffield, and three agents. Also seated at the table were Rex Sampson, Eddie, and his handler Zoe plus Bud, Jack and Bear.

McCormick began, "First, you may question why Mr. Sampson is here. We are going to need some special favors from the city to pull this off and we are hopeful he can arrange their help. Rex is one of the founding partners of the law practice Sampson, Boone, and Holt. He and his firm were heavily involved helping us set up the contractor program for the MSST. They have contributed both financially and professionally. Also, they are extremely motivated to help defeat the criminal elements of the narcotic drug industry. To make Operation Yellow Jacket successful, we need help from the Dallas Police, the Sherriff's Department, and the Dallas Morning news. Nothing illegal, but certainly stretching the truth for a week or two. Mr. Sampson, do you have influence with each of these to meet our needs?"

Rex said, "Well it depends on what you are asking them to do. But if it is reasonable, I can assure you they will do what I ask. After all, the firm has contributed heavily to each of their political campaigns. I guess you could say that we got them elected."

"Okay Rex, I am going to take that as a yes. Now, the next step is to evaluate our undercover agent. Mr. Suffield, is Eddie Mahan ready?"

"I had my doubts at first, but he is truly a quick study. Let me defer your question to his handler, Ms. Zoe Castillo."

Eddie was in full costume as Zoe stood up and asked Bud, "This is Carlos Jekel, a.k.a. Doctor Jekel or just Doc. Can you identify him as your brother?

Bud stared at Eddie and said, "No, my brother does not own a suit. He has grey hair and would never wear a man-bun. May I ask him a question?"

"Sure."

"Eddie, do you know what you are getting into?"

Eddie answered in Spanish, "[Señor, If you are asking me a question, please use my name. I do not know this Eddie.]"

Bud laughed out loud and said, "Okay, I don't recognize this guy. He is a total stranger to me."

Zoe responded, "We are still working on the gang language, but he will be ready in a week."

"Thank you Ms. Castillo, good work."

Howard Suffield remained standing and said, "The DEA and our guys at the FBI have been busy identifying the key players of the cartel and local dealers. I will give you a list of what we have, but in general, it includes:

- The likely second-in-command of the South American cartel is General Perez and is a very high-value target. He watches over most of the supply ships and observes the delivery of the narcotics and the resulting large cash payments. We most likely will not have a chance to capture him as his ships are heavily armed and very elusive.

- A Texas coastal thug that goes by the name Cujo. In Spanish, it means lame or crippled. In dealing with him, remember a wounded animal is dangerous. He is our prime target and has a reward for his capture or death.
- Deuce Rodriquez is a local gang kingpin controlling much of the narcotics trafficking in the Dallas/Ft. Worth Metroplex. He has ambitions to expand into Oklahoma but is currently sitting in the Dallas County jail awaiting trial. In fact, he is the reason we have the opportunity to run the Yellow Jacket sting. We are planning to fake his death and cover his absence by implanting Carlos Jekel to take over his operations.
- Hugo, the Accountant, is Mr. Rodriquez right-hand man and runs most of the drug trafficking duties including repackaging to street size bags and of course, handles the money.
- We could not get all the street captains, but we did identify eight. We estimate there may be three more. These are critical in getting acceptance of the coup. If they run, we lose the power to capture Cujo."

Captain McCormick took control of the meeting and said, "One more thing and we'll take a break. The very first item right now is to plant misinformation with the newspaper. Rex, we need to have an article run in the City-State section this weekend. The article primarily warns the public to watch out for gang violence over the next month. Indicate that the city might be a bit more dangerous as the Cosa Nostra Mafia is rumored to be expanding its operations to the Metroplex. The expected drug wars could spill over to the public. The purpose is to provide credence to our coup. You might also give some notice to the sheriff jail facilities as we will need some help with Deuce Rodriquez.

Rex said, "Consider it done."

"Okay Rex, you may leave or you are welcome to stay. Let's take a fifteen-minute break and come back here to start fleshing out the plan."

As the group began to stand, Rex said, "You know, I think I will stay. It might give some more insight as to what I need to tell the sheriff."

Chapter 29

Within a week, the misinformation effort was working so well several local T.V. stations were doing special interest bulletins on the upcoming drug wars and the Cosa Nostra. The articles included things or places to avoid and generally how to be safe. Following the FBI plan, the sheriff announced the moving of Mr. Deuce Rodriquez to a private cell for security and protection. He stated that they were concerned a prisoner with a possible Cosa Nostra connection might try to assassinate him.

During that week, an FBI agent, disguised as a jailer, began delivering meals to the prisoners who were in isolation or were otherwise outside the general prisoner population. He was friendly and always stayed a few minutes to chat with each inmate. He also carefully monitored the visitor log and as suspected Hugo the Accountant made daily visits to Mr. Rodriquez at precisely two o'clock each afternoon.

The following Monday evening, the agent carefully mixed a powdered form of general anesthesia into Mr. Rodriquez's meal. He chose a drug commonly used for major surgery in many hospitals. It would keep a patient utterly unconscious for four to six hours. The agent drank an ice tea and pulled a chair over to talk to Deuce as he ate his meal. The conversation was friendly and centered on his upcoming trial. They discussed if the judge would let him out on bail. The agent soon said his goodnight and took the empty tray away.

Within fifteen minutes Deuce Rodriquez was in his bed and appeared lifeless. Medics, again FBI, were called in to roll him out on a stretcher and put him in an ambulance for shipment to an emergency room. However, the ambulance transported him to a private prison fifty miles away and placed him in solitary confinement. The Dallas prison population quickly began the rumor that he died of poisoning.

That afternoon, Carlos Jekel was in the visitor lobby when The Accountant came for his daily meeting with his boss.

Sitting in a metal chair wearing gray slacks, a black turtleneck, and a black windbreaker, Carlos said in Spanish, "[Good morning Hugo. Please have a seat here next to my dog. I have some news concerning Deuce Rodriquez that you will need to know.]"

"[Who are you and what have you done with Mr. Rodriquez?]"

"[Please sit, I will tell you all I know.]"

"[Are you the Cosa Nostra? I have heard they are here.]"

"[Ah, Mr. Accountant, you surely don't expect me to answer that question here in the offices of the police.]"

"[What do you want and I will be on my way.]"

"[I am very sorry to inform you that Mr. Rodriquez passed away last night. A heart attack I have been told.]"

Shocked and angered, Hugo demanded, "[I need proof.]"

Carlos motioned to the officer at the front desk and said, "[Easy, just ask the jailer.]"

Hugo rushed to the desk and after a few moments of hushed tones, Hugo's face turned blank and walked back to Carlos, sat down, and asked, "[How did you do it?]"

"[I didn't, but I knew about it.]"

"[What do you want?]"

"[You know what I want. I am sure you have read about it in the newspaper.]"

"[You will never get away with it. Not this easy.]

"[Well, that is why I am here. Let's just call it a merger between two business ventures. Do it my way and we both win. Resist and I will win anyway. The newspaper severely underestimates the violence that will come to you and your little organization. I want to make a deal.]"

"[What kind of deal.]"

"[I want a sit-down meeting with you and all your field captains. I will explain my offer and they can decide for themselves, up or down. You vote to join me and it is even better than you have it now. You vote not to join and I leave to report to my bosses. I will give you until the morning to make up your mind. I have arranged a safe place to meet. Here is a card from my hotel. Call before ten in the morning. Your choices are to confirm you and your gang will be there or I make the call to Philly.]"

"[Yes, I understand. I need some time to check out your story on Deuce Rodriquez.]"

"[I agree. I hope you make the call tomorrow. It costs nothing to listen to my offer.]"

Carlos and Blimey exited the room. The Accountant watched out the window as they entered a huge black Lincoln Town Car staffed with a large bodyguard, a driver, and Zoe Castillo.

After turning the corner, Howard Suffield asked, "How did it go?"

Eddie responded, "You tell me," as he reached over to Blimey and handed the agent the dog tag recorder.

In less than three minutes, they were listing to the entire conversation being interpreted by Zoe. With a smile on his face, Howard said, "Excellent Doc. I think you set the hook."

The hotel room phone rang at 10:01 and as Carlos answered, he motioned Zoe to move near to listen.

The Accountant said in Spanish, "[Yes, we are willing to sit down. Will this be a gun-free meeting?]"

"[It is up to you amigo, just keep all of the guns out of sight. Of course, I will have my bodyguards and my dog.]"

"[Ah yes, your dog.]"

"[I have a banquet room reserved at Junior's Steak House in the downtown warehouse district. Are you familiar with it?]"

"Sí."

"[Be there at two this afternoon, sharp. Use the back entrance and ask for Doc. See you then. Adiós.]"

Zoe translated to Howard, who was also in the room, and added, "It is time to call Rex and tell him to contact his friends at the funeral home rental services."

Smiling at the thought, Howard said, "This will go down as the best decoy ever. We will pick up each hearse at noon. I will have eight agents disguised as funeral drivers."

By one the next afternoon, five FBI agents were scattered around Junior's regular seating area and ordering lunch. They were not part of the meeting, but if things got out of control they would be ready. At ten to two, the black Lincoln was parked and two large and ruffled agents stepped out to escort Carlos and Blimey. Shortly after, Hugo the Accountant led ten unkempt gang-bangers through the kitchen and into the banquet room, sitting them around the table. None were happy to be there.

Eddie thought, *I cannot believe that these scumbags control the sale of narcotics in the entire Metroplex. But they each run maybe a hundred street gangs.*

Carlos, in his two thousand dollar suit, black silk shirt, and the one thousand dollar alligator shoes remained standing next to Blimey. His two bodyguards never sat down.

Checking his watch, Carlos began the meeting in Spanish, "[If you are questioning what happened to Deuce Rodriquez, I can tell you that he is dead. The police think it was either a heart attack or poisoning. The morgue will have its findings in due time. So I guess you are wondering what is going to happen with all your good work.]"

A hand came up and asked, "[Are you Cosa Nostra?]"

"[Sort of.] But before I explain, I want to use English for the remainder of the meeting so that my friends behind me can follow along. Okay, back to your question. Casa Nostra is an Italian crime family primarily located on the East Coast, New York and Philly. The southern version was founded a few years ago in Puerto Rico and is called La Costa Nostra. But the money and power end up at the same place.

"I am Puerto Rican and was noticed by the local mafia there. After a few years, I was moved to Philadelphia and became Cosa Nostra. A few more years and I was selected to become part of The Family. It is called becoming a "Made Man". Do you know what it's like being "Made Man" ? It cannot be any better.

I share the money and get protection. No one can touch me. If you do, you and your family will disappear. My name is Doctor Carlos Jekel, but you must call me Doctor Jekel or just Carlos, at least until we become better friends.

"You have a choice to make today. You vote to join me and it is even better than you have it now. You vote not to join and I leave to report to my bosses. If you do not believe their power, may I make a little demonstration?"

He turns to a bodyguard, "Please hand me the portable phone."

Carlos then holds the phone up for all to see. It was a new 1984 mobile telephone, the first of its kind. It was the size of a building brick and had a flexible antenna sticking out the top.

"Have you ever seen one of these? Just think, you no longer do your business on a pay phone. Join me and you each get one. Now let me demonstrate how it works."

Scanning the table, "Señor Rojo, I have your home number in the speed-dial of the phone. When I push this button, I will call your house. Let's put it on speaker so we can all listen."

A female person answered, "[Hello.]"

"Good afternoon, Señora Rojo, your husband and I are calling. He would like for you to look out your front door and tell us what you see?"

She put the receiver down and went to the window and screamed.

"And what did you see?"

"[A funeral hearse.]"

"Thank you, Señora Rojo. Adiós."

Carlos had everyone's attention.

"That was fun, let's do that again. Mr. Acosta, you are next. This time you talk."

He said when the phone was answered, "It is me. I want you to look outside and tell me what you see."

Over the speaker came a frightened response, "It is a hearse, who is it for?"

Carlos disconnected and said, "Who wants to be next?"

No one answered.

A moment later a small man stood up and said, "[Let me dial my own number.]"

"Certainly," said Carlos as he pushed the phone to him.

His wife quickly answered and shouted, "[Come home, I need you now. There is a hearse out front!]"

Carlos took the phone, disconnected, and gave it to one of the bodyguards, "Call your boys back in, we have seen enough. Bring back every hearse."

"In ten minutes all will be back to normal at your house."

Scanning the room Carlos said, "When you get home tonight, ask your family if they saw a funeral wagon. You now understand I know where you live. If you do not join our effort, we will return in the days ahead to fill up each hearse with whoever we find at your house. I want to vote right now. Either we work together or I start over. Which is it?"

As each hand popped up, they said, "I will join."

Looking over at The Accountant, he said, "Congratulations, you have some smart captains here. Now, I need to talk to Cujo. Call me tonight about what he thinks. I want to meet with him in the morning. We need to arrange a large purchase."

With that, Carlos, Blimey, and the guards left the room and drove off in the Lincoln. As the gang filed out of the restaurant and into the parking lot, their heads were hanging low and looking dazed and confused, but hopeful.

Back at the hotel room they all gathered around and replayed Blimey's recording over and over. Zoe poured a round of cold champagne, but Howard said, "Cujo may be a bit tougher."

Chapter 30

While having breakfast at Denney's near Love Field, Cujo and The Accountant were discussing their options. Unknown to them were a team of FBI agents on a street side listening to their conversation.

Cujo stated in Spanish, "[This looks like a setup. You don't just call a meeting, walk in, and take over a multi-million dollar narcotics operation without spilling some serious blood.]"

The Accountant answered, "[Precisely, I agree, but that is what he did. He gave us a choice of joining Cosa Nostra and continuing our business or dying. Our guys are frightened. The act of parking a hearse in front of each captain's house took away their will to fight. To them, being raided by the cops is better than facing Carlos.]"

"[It all depends if Deuce is in fact dead but we will not know for a while.]"

After a moment to think, The Accountant said, "[We must assume that Carlos is Cosa Nostra. If we go against him and he is, then we most likely will die. If we go against him and he is not, then he is FBI and we get arrested.]"

"[Sí, I agree, but we are very low in inventory and need to make a buy. I suggest we play along with him, take the shipment, and give us some time. Our best plan is to make nice with Carlos, resupply our inventory, and snoop around for Deuce.]"

"[Our standard shipment is forty-five kilos at a dealer price of fifty-four hundred thousand dollars. The Street value is about nine hundred thousand. We have more than enough money in our safe house to make this buy.]"

"[Let's not do anything unusual. We keep this purchase the same and maybe the cartel will not be made aware of our problems. We don't want them to get involved.]"

The Accountant had a look of concern as he asked, "[Where is the supply ship now? We need to make this buy in a few days.]"

"[It's scheduled to be off Galveston in two days. Let's just act normal, but I want to challenge Carlos one time to see how he reacts. If I am satisfied, we go with it.]"

"[How are you going to do that?]"

"[I don't know just yet.]"

"[Meet him this morning. He is expecting you. Here is the hotel card, just ask the hotel desk to connect you to Carlos Jekel.]"

The agents in the van outside did a high-five and made a call to their boss, Howard Suffield, "Cujo is on the way and he will demand proof. Expect a call within thirty minutes."

Early on, the FBI had anticipated that Cujo would ask for some form of assurance and had already devised a plan to address the request. The CIA had an office in San Juan and a week before the coup, they installed a phone line directly to the desk of an agent and coached him to play the boss of the Puerto Rican Cosa Nostra boss. He was to be called Papa and Zoe was to play his LA granddaughter, Nieta. She was to be in charge of the Texas operation.

The call to the room came from the front desk of the hotel, "Doctor Jekel, you have a visitor here in the lobby, a Mister Cujo. Would you want me to send him to your room?"

"Yes, thank you."

A few minutes later a knock on the door and Cujo was escorted into the meeting room of the suite.

Cujo immediately froze at the sight of Eddie, the two FBI agents, Zoe, and Blimey. He reached for his gun and Zoe shouted in Spanish, "[Stop, we are all armed. We are here to do business, not to shoot you.]"

As Cujo relaxed and moved his hand from his gun, he said, "[Okay and who are you?]"

Carlos smiled and said, "[I am sorry. Let me introduce you to my amigos.] Switching to English he used his open hand to motion to the FBI agents, "These two fine gentlemen are my bodyguards, furnished to me from our company in Philly. They do not speak Spanish and get very nervous when they don't understand what you're saying. Now, this young lady goes by la Nieta. She is our boss man's granddaughter. And of course…" pointing to Blimey, "he is my first level of security. Don't you feel more comfortable now?"

Cujo did not smile.

Carlos continued, "Everyone, this is Cujo, the Cocaine King."

Directing his next comment to Cujo, "I think we all would like to know how you became crippled."

Cujo angrily looked at Carlos and stated, "That is not important. I am here to find out who you are and if I am satisfied, we can then talk business."

"You are a very cautious man. I like that. We all need to feel comfortable with our business associates. How can I help?"

"I need some proof that Deuce is dead."

"Ahh, that one is easy. This morning's paper listed Mr. Rodriquez death as a poisoning, and later today, he will be cremated. What else do you need?"

"How can you have a coup with no bloodshed?"

"It is not done yet. I promise you would not like that. What else?"

"Prove you are Cosa Nostra."

"I don't know if I can do that. Let la Nieta handle this one."

Wearing tight black riding pants and knee-high boots with spiked heels and a low cut white top with black trim, she walked toward Cujo placing one foot in front of the other until she was towering over him with her hands on her hips. "Mr. Cujo, if I let you do this, you must promise me that you will show the utmost respect. Papa, my grandfather, is second-in-command of all of Cosa Nostra outside of Italy. His only boss lives in Philly. If you do not show respect to him or me, the bloodshed will start here in this room. Do you understand?"

"Sí, now prove to me."

"Understand, he only takes phone calls from within Cosa Nostra. If he takes this call, you need to be short and to the point. He will hang up in less than two minutes to avoid tracing and tomorrow he will get a new number. Remember, be short and be respectful."

"Sí, let me talk to him."

She placed the phone on speaker so the room could hear her dial the operator and requested to place an international call. After some time the CIA agent answered, "[Papa here.]" His voice was deep and annoyed, "[What is it you need?]"

La Nieta was very apologetic as she explained the reason for the call. She spoke in Spanish, "[I would like to report that your business expansion is going very well and Carlos has done an outstanding task of presenting it to the Dallas people. We are ready to make our first purchase of inventory, but the distributor needs some reassurance that we are who we claim to be. His name is Cujo and he is requesting to speak to you. He is on the speaker phone.]"

Papa replied, "[Mr. Cujo, be careful what you ask. I do not discuss family business over the telephone.]"

Panicked, Cujo looked at la Nieta, "[What name do I use to talk to him?]"

"[Just Papa.]"

Cujo stood tall and addressed the phone, "[Mr. Papa can you confirm that Carlos Jekel is a member of your family?]"

"[I warned you, I do not discuss these things. However, I know Carlos like a brother. I have sent him to Texas to negotiate a trade agreement. If he is not successful, I am afraid that he will be coming to your funeral within thirty days. Nice talking to you Mr. Cujo, hope to be doing business with you.]"

"[With all due respect Mr. Papa, that did not prove anything but a threat.]"

The response from Papa was cold and angry, "[No Mr. Cujo, it is you that must prove to me that you can supply the product we need. If not, a replacement will take over. Permanently. Capisci?]"

The next sound from the phone was a dial-tone.

Zoe put the receiver down, looked at Cujo and speaking in English, "That is as good as you are going to get. Do we have a deal or not?"

"I am cautious, but I am satisfied, I will arrange the purchase. The supply ship is two days away. Meet me at my boat at 9:00 AM, the day after tomorrow."

Carlos broke in, "Where will we meet you?"

"It is docked at the Shrimp Haven Marina, down in Freeport, Texas. It is about eighty miles southwest of Galveston, slip A-8. It is an old Hatteras Yacht named *Golden Nugget*, how much do you want to buy?"

"At least as much as the normal purchase, maybe more. I will need to talk to The Accountant to confirm."

"Bring cash, you have that much don't you?"

"Don't worry about the money. This transaction will be the start of an excellent business deal. Now my bodyguards will escort you out of the hotel. Have The Accountant call me soon."

Shortly Hugo the Accountant called to confirm the deal.

Carlos said, "Meet me in my hotel room to discuss the arrangements and our new partnership. Collect all the cash from the street captains and bring it with you so that we can make the new purchase. We are going to add to that cash to increase the size of the normal amount."

Chapter 31

The FBI Dallas field office was working on the details of the final strategy meeting. Captain McCormick, the boys, Bud, Eddie, and Zoe were there. FBI Field Director Howard Suffield led the presentation.

"Well folks looks like this is it. Everything is in place and coming together. The supply ship should be near Galveston in international waters the day after tomorrow. The purpose of this evening's meeting is to make any last minute adjustments and finalize the capture plans. Let me start with updating current facts."

He had everyone's attention and most were taking notes.

"Operation Yellow Jacket is good-to-go with the drug buy. Hugo The Accountant is cooperating. He has delivered the money. He and Cujo have agreed that the transfer will be for fifty kilos of cocaine at twelve thousand dollars per kilo for six hundred thousand dollars. He will ride down to Freeport with Cujo. Meet us at his boat and will stay at the marina with our agents while waiting for the return of the drugs. If our plan works, Cujo and the boat will not make it back but will be in Coast Guard custody. At that time, The Accountant will be arrested along with a massive raid to round up all the field captains. If something goes wrong at sea and Cujo's boat returns, we will not show our hand but continue with the Operation until further notice."

Sheffield paused and looked at everyone, then continued, "If the capture of Cujo goes well, we will then try to lure or chase the supply ship back into the twelve-mile limit and the Coast Guard will attempt a capture. Everyone with me so far?"

All nodded their head in the affirmative.

On the conference table was an aluminum device not much larger than a big box of kitchen matches and a threaded hole in either side.

The director picked it up for all to see and said, "Now, for tonight's assignment. The FBI technical shop has built a fuel cutoff valve. It is to be installed on Cujo's boat tonight. It fits on the fuel line between the fuel tank and the engines. Think of it as a garage door opener. It will be controlled by a remote, which is made to look like the hotel key, and carried on to the boat by Carlos.

"No doubt, they will search Carlos for weapons or a recorder, but they should not care about his room key. On the return from the supply ship, just inside the twelve-mile line, Carlos will use the remote to activate the valve which will turn off the fuel and stop the engines. Cujo will be hesitant to use the marine radio to ask for help and risk Coast Guard involvement and he certainly would not want the supply ship to know about his breakdown."

Howard chuckled and continued, "Our salvage and repair ship, the *Castaway*, will just happen to be nearby on a fake repair job and conveniently notices Cujo's stranded boat. *Castaway* will move over to offer help and Bear will board Cujo's boat. At that time, we will have the advantage of superior weapons and the shock of surprise. This situation should allow us to hold the boat until the Coast Guard can come over for the arrest."

"Any questions?"

"How do we get the valve installed?"

"You will need to figure that out. We will have an agent there at the marina to watch the boat. If it's vacant, it will be an easy job for Bear. I suggest you use scuba gear to avoid suspicious eyes. Once the installation is complete, you retreat to your boat and wait for morning. You will leave the ship channel at sun up and wait for Cujo to move out. Captain McCormick, do you have anything to add?"

"Yes, just a few items. The decoy boat will follow *Castaway*. We will be using encrypted communications with you while we track the position of Cujo.

When his vessel becomes stranded, you will motor over to check if they need assistance. You will explain that you are just finishing a repair of a water pump on the other boat. Any questions?"

Bud asked, "Do we show that we are armed?"

"Good question. No, we don't want to spook Cujo. He will be in a stressful condition anyway and we all know he can be very aggressive. Also, this is an excellent time to reinforce your rules of engagement. You may not use lethal force unless you are threatened or feel the situation will escalate to a danger level. Also, you should always have the com gear working for each person on the boat. Obviously, this does not apply to Eddie."

Captain McCormick and group returned to the Houston Coast Gard station. Jack and crew immediately began preparing to make the short trip to Freeport.

Castaway was on her way within an hour and heading south. A quarter moon was out when they settled into a calm anchorage on the edge of the Intercoastal Waterway, a mile from the Shrimp Haven Marina. Bear opened the deck doors and assembled the crane to lift the inflatable dinghy and the outboard motor into the water. Bud watched from the *Castaway*'s bridge as the boys moved the scuba gear into the small boat. Another fifteen minutes and they had tied the dinghy to an old post near the marina. It only took a few minutes to adjust the scuba gear and they were in the water heading for slip A-8 and the *Golden Nugget*.

They were still in the water and evaluating their next step, as they heard a man's voice say, "You are safe, come on out of the water."

Jack asked, "Do you know Howard Sheffield?"

"He's my boss."

"Great. Come on Bear, it's time to get to work."

"Yeah, but be careful, the boat has a guard. He left about thirty minutes ago. If he returns, I will try to distract him."

Jack looked over at Bear, as he was already opening the engine room door and on his way down. Using a flashlight and tools he brought, it took only a few minutes to install and test the valve. As Bear was beginning to open the door to exit, Jack heard the agent talking very loudly.

"How you doing, mate?" asked the agent with a slight slur to his words. "Come have a cold beer with me."

Jack realized that the agent was talking to the guard.

"Come on, mate. I hate to drink alone."

"I can't, I must watch the boat for my boss."

"My boat is right over here. You can watch from there. I have some cold ones iced down and a pizza," he reached over and gave the guard a beer.

"Okay, I am having a hard time staying awake sitting here by myself anyway."

"Excellent, follow me."

By the time the agent and the guard were on the other boat and settling down, Jack and Bear were back in the water and making their return to *Castaway*. Bud enjoyed hearing about the agent and the guard as the boys cleaned and stored their scuba gear and secured the inflatable back into the hull of *Castaway*. The rest of the night, they each stood watch for three hours and was on their way by sunup. Bud noticed the decoy boat was following them out to open water.

A little before 9:00 AM, the agent called Howard and reported that Cujo and The Accountant had just pulled in the marina parking lot. Shortly afterward, the big Lincoln arrived. All exited their cars and stretched their legs as Carlos, wearing grey slacks, a Hawaiian shirt, and deck shoes, looked at Cujo and started the conversation, "Nice day for a sail."

Cujo answered, "This is not a pleasure trip. Did you bring the money?"

One of the agents walked over to the Lincoln, popped the trunk, reached in, and pulled out a large suitcase. Lugging it over to Cujo's car, he lifted it onto the hood, unlatched the top, and opened it.

Cujo picked up several banded stacks of one hundred dollar bills and grinned, "Well, I guess you did."

The agent snatched the money from Cujo and returned it to the suitcase. Where do you want me to put it?"

"Leave it right there. Carlos will take it."

He added, "No bodyguards on the boat. Just me and Carlos."

Carlos demanded, "And what about your bodyguard? Is he staying here too?"

"No, He is the driver."

"Okay with me, I will just bring my dog."

Cujo glared at Carlos and demanded, "I must search you before we board. No weapons or a wire."

"Then I must also search you."

Neither found weapons, but Cujo did notice Carlos' room key. He let him keep it.

On the way out, Cujo and Carlo discussed business issues and during the conversation, Cujo, now speaking Spanish mentioned Deuce, "[Carlos, I cannot believe you killed him.]"

"[It was the easiest way. Saved a lot of blood.]"

"[I agree with that. He would have fought you to the death. He was one bad ass kind of hombre.]"

"[Is that correct? I heard that he had a violent temper.]"

Cujo answered, "Sí."

"[I heard that he was a killer?]"

"Sí. [For sure. I know of four that I watched. All gang-related, either used the drugs themselves or tried to keep the money.]"

"[I guess that does officially make him a bad ass hombre.]"

Eddie reached over to scratch Blimey behind his ears and thought, *I hope you recorded that conversation.*

Chapter 32

Using the encrypted radio, Captain McCormick informed Jack, "Go ahead and start using your com gear and be sure to put on your bulletproof vests. We need to start monitoring all activity now. Plus, remember you are a commercial repair boat, so do not change to the camo mode for this stage of the sting.

"The *Golden Nugget* has left the marina. They should reach open water within thirty minutes. We will be using the Coast Guard cutter *Eagle* to be the command center. It has long-range radar capable of tracking you, the decoy boat, and Cujo's boat. Right now, we can see out past the twelve-mile limit and can identify three ships that are in the area where we expect to find the supply vessel. Set a temporary course due south at thirty knots. We will keep you posted with changes as they happen."

"Rodger."

It was a beautiful day to be on the water, calm seas, southeast winds at five to ten knots, and temperatures in the eighties. A perfect day for Operation Yellow Jacket.

Nearing international waters, Captain McCormick called again, "You should begin to see a cluster of offshore platforms on your starboard bow. Idle-down there and wait for my command."

"Roger, I can see the platforms. Will do."

Both *Castaway* and the decoy boat stopped to await directions. Bear was staring at the largest of the structures and questioned, "Hey Jack, isn't this where we saw the big sharks when we first brought Castaway home?"

"Maybe it is. I'll check the charts, I believe I marked it." After a few moments he said, "Yeah Bear, you're correct. While we are waiting, we'll ease over to see if they are still there. Do we have any food in the fridge?"

"Give me a minute and I will go down and look."

"Bear, you were correct. I can see some shark fins moving out to check us out now."

"Well, we only have a package of chips down here. I am coming back up."

Bud casually said, "Looks like they're hungry."

Two hours had passed since Cujo left the marina and he was now in international waters. He picked up the marine radio mic and said in Spanish, "[Amigo, this is *Golden Nugget*. Over.]"

The reply was a single number, "Cinco."

Cujo retrieved a note card, and said to his driver, "[Number five.]" Showing the card to the driver and pointing to the fifth note, he said, "[Change your heading to this location.]"

Captain McCormick keyed his headset and informed *Castaway*, "Cujo has made contact with the supply ship and is now on a new bearing. We now have a target located. Hold your position."

Within thirty minutes, Cujo located a large sport-fishing yacht sitting motionless. It had a couple of fishing poles on either side with lines in the water. The driver circled to the rear of the yacht and confirmed the name on the transom, then cautiously moved to the port side of *Inca Jewel* and yelled out in Spanish, "[Ahoy, where do you want me to tie up?]"

The captain of the yacht was up in the flybridge with an AK-47 pointed down at Cujo, "[All of you, put your hands up.]"

The driver, Cujo, and Carlos immediately complied. When the captain was satisfied, he gave an all-clear sign to his partners below. Another three bodyguards came out of the cabin, each banishing AK-47s. Shortly, after assurances it was safe, General Perez stepped out and smiled, "[Welcome Cujo and who do you have with you?]"

"[I am sorry I did not contact you sooner, but this is our new leader, Carlos Jekel, of the Cosa Nostra.]"

"[I like Cosa Nostra. What happened to Deuce Rodriquez? I liked him too.]"

"[He was killed while in prison. Carlos and his organization are taking over.]"

"[As long as he has the cash and increases our sales, I will be happy to do business with Mr. Jekel.]"

"Sí. [For sure. We are already increasing our normal order. We need fifty kilos of cocaine at twelve thousand dollars per kilo. That amounts to six hundred thousand dollars.]"

Another big smile from the General, "[My men will load the bags. Will you like to test the quality of the merchandise, before I count the money?]"

Carlos responded, "[No, I will trust Cujo. If we determine that you have supplied less that you have promised, we will end our relationship with Cujo and you too General Perez.]"

"[Are you threatening me?]"

"[Oh no. It is not a threat, it is a fact. Do you want to count the money now?]"

"Sí. [I am not as trusting as you.]"

"[Then have your men carry this suitcase to your boat. Once you are satisfied, we will be on our way.]"

"Sí. [We have many more stops to make this week.]"

In ten minutes, they were untying the lines and releasing the two boats. General Perez stepped outside to wave at Cujo and Carlo, "Adios amigos."

Captain McCormick keyed his headset, "Jack, the purchase was successful and Cujo is returning. Looks as if he is heading directly toward you. Get ready to set up with the decoy boat. Eddie will stop the engines as soon as he can identify you. Good luck."

Jack thought, *No telling what may happen. We should prepare for a fight. We will not wear weapons in the open, but we will lay them out on the decks for easy reach.*

Cujo and the driver took the easy way home which was to backtrack the route they used coming out. Eddie went up to the flybridge to watch for the first glimpse of *Castaway* and within a half hour, he spotted the two boats near the offshore platforms. He casually went down to talk to Cujo to avoid suspicion. They were enjoying a cold beer and celebrating the successful transaction when Eddie put his hand in his pocket and secretly toggled the button on his room key.

Both engines stopped with Cujo looking at Carlos and then up to the driver, "[Are we out of gas?]"

"[No, the gauge is reading half full.]"

"[Go down and see if you can find the trouble.]"

After a few minutes of fumbling around and the driver shouted out, "[I see nothing.]"

Cujo looked at Carlos and said, "[I cannot use the marine radio. The Coast Guard may come out, or worse, General Perez will hear and think me a fool.]"

"[Let me borrow your binoculars. I think I might see some help.]"

"[What is it?]"

"[It is a repair boat. We need a way to attract attention.]"

"Cujo said, "Quick driver, go up and honk the ship's horn. Let me have the binoculars.]"

After several attempts, Cujo said, "Sí. [The repair boat is coming to assist. I must go down and out of sight. I am a wanted man.]"

Shortly, *Castaway* was alongside the *Golden Nugget*. Jack was down on the back deck and shouted out, "You guys need some help?"

Carlos shouted back, "Yes, both engines have stopped."

"Are you out of fuel?"

"No, we already checked that."

"Sounds like a fuel filter." Pointing to the decoy boat, he continued, "We just finished a water pump job. Let me tie up and I will send my mechanic over to check you out."

"Okay. Driver, go tell Cujo the good news."

Bear stepped over onto the deck of the *Golden Nugget*, anticipating an easy takedown.

However, Cujo immediately exploded out of the cabin with a gun in his hand, shouting, "Hector Gomez! I have been looking for you for a year. I can't believe you are here on my boat. What a great day as I am finally going to get to kill you."

Everyone on both boats froze for an instant.

Eddie stepped toward Cujo and said in a calm voice, "Be careful, you have witnesses."

Cujo was now worked up into a crazed frenzy, turned to look at Jack and shouted, "We will kill them all and take their boat."

While Cujo was looking at Jack, Bear stepped closer and Blimey moved next to Bear and began barking and growling.

The driver also stepped down to the deck in anticipation of a fight.

Cujo swung the gun back to Bear and snarled, "You did this to me. You made me a cripple and you must die!"

As he lifted the gun to aim, Blimey hurled himself toward Cujo and clamped down on his wrist, causing the weapon to discharge into the air and fall to the deck. Bear was close enough to deliver a left uppercut to Cujo's chest followed by a right cross to his jaw.

The force of Bear's punches lifted Cujo up and into the water, causing a massive splash. Cujo began to yell, "Help me, I cannot swim."

From *Castaway*'s bridge, Bud yelled down while pointing towards the back of the boat, "I don't think drowning is your problem. Look at the shark fins!"

Frightened, Cujo turned just in time to see the first shark grab his leg and pull him under water. As most of the attention was on the attack, Jack picked up the M-4 Assault Rifle and looked over at the driver.

The driver had Cujo's gun and was pointing it at Bear. He shouted, "I should have shot you the same time I shot your mother."

Before he could pull the trigger, Jack put a three round burst into the driver's chest, knocking him over the aft rail and landing on the swim platform.

Not knowing the platform was there, Bear was sure he was in the water and was stunned to see a hand reach over the rail to try to grasp for leverage. In a rage, Bear moved to the edge and saw the driver looking up at him with fear in his eyes.

Bear said, "Go burn in hell you son-of-a-bitch!" Then reached down to grab the driver's hand and began to pull him up over the rail.

At that instant, the water began to boil as a shark grabbed his foot and began to shake. No matter how hard Bear pulled, he could not lift both the driver and the shark. At this time, another monster shark launched up on the swim platform and grabbed the driver around the waist.

Bear continued to pull until Eddie stepped over and put his hand on Bear's shoulder, "Let him go. He is already dead."

Bear released the hand and watched the sharks fight over body parts.

The sharks did quick work as they took the bodies underwater. The only sign of Cujo and the driver was the red tint surrounding the boats.

Somberly Bear and Eddie climbed back on the deck of *Castaway*. Jack keyed his headset and asked Captain McCormick, "Did you get that?"

"Yes, you guys did what you had to. Good job."

"The fuel valve is back to normal and the engines are working. You need to helicopter a captain over here to take the boat. We are now transitioning to Camo and going after General Perez. Give me the coordinates.

Chapter 33

Keying his lip mic, Captain McCormick said, "Roger that Jack, Let me check the radar." After a few moments he continued, "Okay, it looks like *Inca Jewel* did not notice your takedown of the *Golden Nugget.* They are on a steady easterly course at thirty knots. If you take a southeastern heading at forty-five knots, you should intercept in about an hour. I will monitor your course and get back to you with final numbers when your closer."

"Roger Captain, we are going to change into the camo mode and put on our disguises. Refer to our boat now as *Revenge*. Wish you could see us. We would scare the crap out of anyone at a Halloween party."

"Ha, you guys are scary enough as you are. Good luck."

Jack set the autopilot and keyed his mic for all to hear and said, "Keep Blimey in the tower, they will recognize him. We have just over thirty minutes to intercept. I am changing to the camo mode. Bear, take down the U.S. flag and put up the skull and crossbones. Everyone, change into your disguise and get the weapons out and ready. I expect a battle."

Pulling the costume box out of storage, Bear sorted and spread out each disguise on the beds. Eddie needed the most help with his assembly. He stripped down to his underwear and put on the bulletproof Kevlar vest and upper arm protection. The next step was to apply black makeup around his eyes and install red contacts. Jack and Bear helped wrap his legs, body, arms, and head with white medical gauze and secured the pieces in place with white duct tape. They carefully took the time to leave space over his eyes to be able for him to see. All agreed he looked like a mummy with a hangover. He finished with new SWAT boots and a World War One army helmet which was made bulletproof with a Kevlar lining.

Bear's costume was the easiest to assemble. He wore a Kevlar vest and arm protection, which Marge had colored and padded to look like an Olympic weightlifter, with super abs and massively muscled arms. He topped off the costume with Japanese Samurai Warrior pants that bloomed out and tucked into his boots. Bear made his head protection by starting with a football helmet and screwing metal around the outside making it into a face mask. It looked like something out of *Mad Max*. The last piece was old World War One tank goggles with dark lenses.

SEAL team combat pants were Jack's start. To this, he added the Kevlar protection which Marge had painted with tan flesh tones and added many prison tattoos covering his body and both arms. On top of the vest, he put on football shoulder pads which remained exposed. A spooky hockey mask was next. For his head, he wore a long blond braided wig and a modified SEAL team helmet, adding broom like blond hair sticking straight up like a Mohawk hairstyle. The last touch was the red contacts.

Bud had always dreamed of being a pirate, so he chose to wear one of the costumes that the boys bought in Charleston. It had a big blousy white shirt and black, loose-fitting pants tucked into combat boots and were held up with a traditional broad black belt with a silver belt buckle. Of course, he had a bulletproof vest and Kevlar lining in the feathered, large felt pirate hat. Marge finished off his outfit with a black wig that hung to his shoulders and a bushy black mustache. She also had added a mouthpiece painted to look like he was missing half his teeth.

Jack checked his radar and noticed two vessels ten miles ahead. He keyed his lip mic and said, "Captain McCormick, I need some help. I have two targets dead ahead."

"Roger, we are looking at that now. It could be another narcotics drop. Hold your position and we will keep you posted."

A few minutes had passed and the captain called back, "Looks like it was just a passing ship. *Inca Jewel* is heading east, the other vessel has passed and continued south. Go ahead and pursue our target. Let me know when you have a visual. For your info, he is into international waters by four miles."

"Roger."

Bear was the first to catch a glimpse of a boat, "Jack, look about ten degrees to starboard."

"Yea, I can just make it out. Check the binoculars."

Captain McCormick keyed back in, "You should be able to see him now."

"Affirmative."

"Approach him from the stern. We want to make sure it's *Inca Jewel.*"

"Agree."

"After confirming identification, try to force him north into U.S. waters. If he doesn't come to us, you will have to confront him to surrender. Expect a fight."

"We are ready, bring it on."

"Don't let him sucker you. If he acts like you kicked his ass, do not set foot on his boat. We have found that most smugglers have their ship wired with explosives. They would prefer to blow up everything, including themselves, and you than to get caught. Do not board the boat unless you must and watch for wire trips.

"Roger, I understand."

"Okay. Good luck, you are on your own."

"Got it, We will bring you some Inca jewelry."

Jack keyed his mic to address his team, "You heard that, we are in the big leagues now. Just for review, Bud will be our driver, Bear is on the bow, Eddie on the rear, and I am a rover. Remember, we cannot shoot first unless we are in danger. Okay Bud, kick this war machine in the ass and get to the rear of that boat to confirm its *Inca Jewel.* If it is, keep about fifty yards out, but come up even with them. Let's go!"

In less than ten minutes they were one hundred yards from the boat. Using the binoculars, Bud confirmed that it was, in fact, *Inca Jewel*, "Okay boys here we go. I am pulling even with them."

Inca Jewel's captain was driving from the flybridge and a guard was with him. He looked over to his right and was surprised to see another boat. They pointed at the new visitor and shouted, "[What is that?]"

"[Looks like a military boat, but it has a pirate flag.]"

"[Could it be a ghost ship?]"

"Sí. Fantasma."

"[Shoot one on them and see if you can kill it.]"

The guard picked up his AK-47 and shot several times at the ghost on the bow. Of the ten or so rounds he fired, one hit Bear and knocked him down to the deck.

Jack ran forward and keyed his mic, "Bear is down, pull us out of here."

He found Bear struggling to breathe and shouted, "Where did you get hit?"

"In the chest, it knocked the shit out of me. Thank God for the Kevlar vest. I'll be okay as soon as I can catch my breath."

Jack keyed the mic, "Bear is good, but I guess we can officially call it a dangerous show of lethal force. Bud, go around again but give us a little more distance. The AK-47s are not very accurate at long range. As soon as we get back in place, let the flybridge have a taste of the fifty-caliber machine guns."

Bud accelerated and was back in position in less than five minutes.

Jack yelled, "Keep firing at the flybridge until I tell you to stop."

With each machine gun firing at five hundred times per minute, they had hit the flybridge with over two thousand rounds in two minutes when Jack finally called a halt. After the barrage was over, the scene was eerily quiet and smoky. Almost nothing was there, no antenna, no radar, no wheel or throttles, no seats and no humans.

General Perez panicked and shouted to the remaining guards, "[We must run. Take control of the boat from the main cockpit, full speed back home. I think we can outrun that bucket of bolts.]"

Inca Jewel accelerated past thirty-five knots and leveled off at just under forty.

Bud announced through the headset, "They're running. We will scoot in front of them and force a turn back to the north."

With the throttles at full speed and smooth seas, they reached almost fifty knots. Making a long loop, soon they were positioned between *Inca Jewel* and South America.

Bud cut back the throttles to idle and waited.

Inca Jewel was charging fast like a bull directly to a matador. Bud waited for General Perez to veer off to avoid a collision, but it seemed intent to ram *Revenge*. At the last minute, Bud accelerated, missing the charging *Inca Jewel* by a few feet.

Jack said, "They will not turn, we must shut down the engines. Bear, where do we shoot to disable the power plant?"

"From the rear of the boat, just above the water line. If that doesn't work, we will need to pull along both sides and shoot halfway between the rail and the water line. Try the rear first."

"Bud responded, "I'm on it."

As *Revenge* caught back up to *Inca Jewel,* Bear grabbed the machine gun, and Jack squatted behind the railing with his M-4 Assault Rifle. One of the guards stepped out of the cabin with his AK-47.

Jack shouted to Bear, "I got this one, you shoot at the engines." He selected the fully automatic mode and began spraying rounds at the guard. Both boats were bouncing causing his shots to be erratic, but one round found the guard in the chest, killing him instantly.

With no further interference, Bear began pounding the transom of *Inca Jewel* with a barrage of fifty-caliber projectiles. Holes opened which allowed him to see the drivetrains. Shortly one engine stopped and then the other. Bud dodged the quickly-slowing *Inca Jewel* and eased up to the side. Both machine guns and the assault rifle pointed at the main cabin. The first sight of movement was the waving of a white towel tied to a fishing pole. The guard stumbled out and held his hands up shouting, "No más, no más."

He pointed to Bear and said, "Espíritu! [Ghost!]"

Bear looked over at Jack and said, "I guess he doesn't like Halloween."

Jack said back to Bear, "Ask him about General Perez."

Bear asked and replied to Jack, "Wounded. Very bad."

"Tell him to drag him out on the deck so we can see."

In a few moments, the general was propped up against the rail and was grasping his hip with blood covering his fingers. Bud climbed down from the tower with a first aid kit and did the best he could to stop the bleeding.

Looking over at Jack, he said, "He needs help."

Jack told Bud to be aware of trip wires, but assess the ship's condition. After a look down in the engine room, Bud reported, "*Inca Jewel* is in trouble."

"Is it sinking?"

"Yes, it will sink if we let it set here. Water is gushing in from the holes in the transom. But if we pull it fast enough the water will drain out. It is just like leaving the drain plug out in a ski boat. Go fast enough to get the nose up and the water will be forced out."

Jack keyed his lip mic for all to hear. "Okay, here is the plan. Bud, pull our boat around and you and Eddie tie a towline on the bow of *Inca Jewel*. Bear, get our new friend to set in the fighting chair and secure him with duct tape. You'll need to ride with them on the way in and if either tries to move, shoot them. I am going back to *Revenge* and monitor the towing."

Eddie threw Bear some of his white duct tape and they were ready in minutes.

Jack keyed his mic, "Captain McCormick, did you copy our plans?"

"Yes, excellent. Set a course to the Northeast. We will meet you at the twelve-mile limit."

"I don't think we can make more than fifteen knots with the tow. Should be there in an hour or so. You need to get prepared to install floatation gear to *Inca Jewel*. She will start to sink when we stop."

"Getting it ready now. We will be waiting."

General Perez continued to bleed and had died by the time they reached the Coast Guard. His bodyguard was still mumbling about devils and the ghost ship.

Captain McCormick came over to *Revenge* and stepped aboard. With a giant smile, he aggressively shook the hands of all and said, "What a perfect ending to Operation Yellow Jacket. Congratulations. We'll take it from here. Head on back to the Swordfish and I will settle up with you guys in a couple of weeks."

Eddie reached down to Blimey and took off the collar-recorder. "I know you will need this. It should tell the whole story and I think it will convict Deuce Rodriquez on four counts of murder."

"I hope so. I am thrilled."

It took some time to clean up the mess and change back to the *Castaway* mode. Still dressed in costume, all climbed up the tower to the bridge and stood in silence as Bud cranked the engines and pointed west. Bear was the first to crack a smile as he went downstairs to the kitchen and came back with two cold six-packs of Coors beer. That ended the silence.

The trip home took twelve hours.

Chapter 34

Rex Sampson and the entire Mahan family were enjoying mid-morning coffee when the lazy sounds of the seagulls were interrupted as Captain McCormick made a low pass over the marina in the HH-65 Dolphin helicopter.

Bud stood up and said, "I think our check is here."

He was carrying a briefcase as he stepped into the café. Cheers, hoots, and whistles erupted as he walked to the table and sat down.

"I think you are going to like this."

Blimey happily barked and wagged his tail.

He opened his case and pulled a large file. "Let me just start with an assessment of damages. To generalize, we effectively shut down the large-scale illegal distribution of narcotics in most of Texas. The Houston area was not hit in this operation, but it is going to be very difficult for drugs to get to the dealers as we shut down their source. The Houston police and FBI are aggressively moving in on them now. Overall, we have won this one, but the demand for narcotics will continue. However, the regular supply route will no longer be the Gulf of Mexico."

Everyone clapped and then Rex stood up and said, "Thank you all. I feel grateful. Thank you."

Captain McCormick continued, "Now for specifics." He pulled out his notes. As for the characters, starting from the top..." He read from a file:

- *"South American cartel General Perez: Dead.*
- *Four South American cartels bodyguards: Three dead, one insane and hospitalized.*
- *Cujo and his bodyguard: Dead.*
- *Deuce Rodriquez: Awaiting trial on four counts of murder and drug trafficking.*
- *Hugo, the Accountant: in jail.*
- *Eight low-level street captains: in jail.*
- *Golden Nugget: Captured with twenty-five kilos of cocaine.*
- *Inca Jewel Captured with six hundred thousand dollars in cash and two hundred kilos of cocaine."*

Captain McCormick looked up and eyed everyone, "Quite an afternoon's work. Gentlemen, now for the fun part." As he opened another file, he itemized:

- "Reward for General Perez: one million dollars
- Reward for Cujo: one hundred thousand dollars
- Recapture of six hundred thousand in cash earns a ten percent fee of sixty thousand dollars
- Capture of two hundred and fifty kilos which at street value of twenty thousand per kilo is five million dollar and earns a fee of twenty percent, or one million dollars."

He then said, "Are you ready for the grand total?"

All of them stood up, "Hell yes!"

He reached into the briefcase, pulled out a check, and snapped it around so all could see. It read "$2,160,000".

The room fell silent.

After the shock wore off, Captain McCormick gathered his briefcase and said, "Be sure to keep up the salvage and repair work going, we might need you guys again. Remember, your company will continue to be a contractor and its monthly fees will be paid."

He boarded the HH-65 Dolphin, strapped himself into the captain's chair, and soon pointed the craft to Houston.

Back at the table, Rex said, "I'll leave it to you guys to decide what to do with the money, but the IRS will want their share. After it settles down, I will get with my guys to file the correct paperwork. One more time, I am very proud of what you accomplished. I am incredibly pleased with my involvement with you guys. I need to get back to work. Goodbye and thanks once again."

Marge said, "According to my calculations, I divided the total by seven and got $308,571.43. The boat receives three shares or $925,714 and each of you will get about $250,000 after taxes. Does anyone want a cold beer?"

Epilogue

Sitting in the dune-buggy and looking out at the surf, I began to feel a nice mood settling in as the sun warms my back.

Looking over at Blimey in the other seat, he has a big smile on his face, with his tongue dangling out the side of his mouth and I said to him, "Finally got to hang out on the beach with my best buddy. Can't get much better.

"We were supposed to be making a career out of beachcombing, but whoever would have guessed my world would get so complicated that I now need a tax attorney? I didn't even ask for it. Oh well, shit happens. Just what can I do with two hundred and fifty thousand dollars? I don't need a damn thing. I'll have plenty of room at the beach house with Dad leaving. I can't believe that Zoe Castillo has taken a month-long leave of absence from the FBI to go sailing with him. I don't know if she is in love with Eddie Mahan or Carlos Jekel. Being trapped with him and two other smelly men on a sailboat with no privacy, she should find out pretty quickly. I wonder if they have a makeup mirror on the boat. Plus, I don't think the group even knows where they are going next. That will be interesting.

"Contrast that with Uncle Bud. He would be happy staying here and looking for another high-stakes poker game. But instead, he is taking Marg on a month-long tour of Europe. Can you just see him trying to get the French to understand his West Texas accent? Even if they could speak English, they will have no idea of what he is saying. Now that I think about it, even the English will be equally bewildered. Speaking of Bud and Marge, it looks like you, me, and Maria will be looking after the Swordfish until they return. Thank God for the offseason.

"Now that leaves Bear. Blimey, do you know that big lug went directly to the Harley dealership and bought the biggest hog they offer?

"Said he was going to see his foster mom, Mrs. Philip. He said that he now has no reason to keep his identity secret. He also told me that he was going to pay off her house and then ride all the way to Ft. Myers, Florida. You know, he never mentioned to me if he intends to return. I guess we'll find out when his money runs dry.

"That is all I know, Blimey. Let's go fishing."

CPSIA information can be obtained
at www.ICGtesting.com
Printed in the USA
FSHW011002250219
55923FS